Praise for *Camp Outlook*:

"Wow! What an exceptional voice. From the opening pages, you'll fall in love with Shan, the wonderful, wise, brave protagonist of this wonderful, wise, brave novel. I couldn't put *Camp Outlook* down – I laughed with Shannon, cried with her, and saw the world through her eyes when the book was done. Brenda Baker writes with great fluidity and poise, tackling big issues with humour, skill and page-turning plot. Terrific."
—Alice Kuipers, author of *Life on the Refrigerator Door* and *40 Things I Want To Tell You*

"*Camp Outlook* is a book that will make you smile 'like you've swallowed the sun.' It will also make your heart ache. Baker's brilliance as a writer is evident in every sentence. She tackles a tough situation with great sensitivity, infuses it with light and is never didactic. Shannon is one fiercely honest, funny, reflective, unsentimental character. Shipped away to church camp because her parents need some space, she unravels her tale. We fall a lot in love with her and the world she's discovering. This is simply one of the best books I've read in a very long time."
—Sheree Fitch, author of *The Gravesavers*

Camp Outlook

Camp Outlook

BRENDA BAKER

Second Story Press

Library and Archives Canada Cataloguing in Publication

Baker, Brenda, 1959-, author
Camp Outlook / by Brenda Baker.

Issued in print and electronic formats.
ISBN 978-1-927583-35-7 (pbk.)

I. Title.

PS8553.A373C36 2014   jC813'.54   C2014-900153-3

C2014-900154-1

Edited by Kathryn Cole
Designed by Melissa Kaita

Cover photo © iStockphoto

Printed and bound in Canada

*Second Story Press gratefully acknowledges the support of the
Ontario Arts Council and the Canada Council for the Arts for our
publishing program. We acknowledge the financial support of the
Government of Canada through the Canada Book Fund.*

MIX
Paper from
responsible sources
FSC
www.fsc.org   FSC® C004071

Published by
Second Story Press
20 Maud Street, Suite 401
Toronto, ON M5V 2M5
www.secondstorypress.ca

For Tori and Tanaya,
and for those who've experienced the love
of an exceptional sibling.

Chapter 1

I'm not crazy. Lots of people see unusual things, and they aren't all called crazy. Take Jesus, for instance. He saw unusual things. Nobody calls him crazy.

And genuine crazies behave weirdly in public. I don't. Mentally, I'm just fine. What I'm going to tell you sounds crazy, but I've thought a lot about it. Obsessed over it. And kept it to myself. Like when I became an atheist for the first time.... And for the second time. I kept that to myself too.

When you're turning into an adult, that's one of the things you have to learn. To keep certain particular things to yourself. Dad calls it "using discretion," which will help you avoid "errors in judgment" that will lead to "inappropriate behavior." He and my mom have been working on these aspects of my upbringing for some time now.

So. I *used discretion* about being an atheist because I didn't want to stick out at school. Like Malcolm Wright, the only other atheist I know. He was already abnormal because he's such a genius science-guy. But when you're twelve and you announce to your class that God doesn't exist, then you're *really* abnormal. People look at you funny and talk behind your back. When his parents made a big stink about us singing Christmas carols in class, that was *major* abnormal, even if our school *is* non-religious. The truth is lots of kids believe in God and such things as going to heaven. (Before I became an atheist, I didn't believe in heaven. Even though my parents go to church, they don't believe in heaven either.) A few kids at school also believe in hell, and they said Malcolm Wright would end up there, even if one day he won the Nobel Prize for curing cancer. How dumb is that?

These kids probably have underdeveloped brains. Kids' brains actually go through different stages. I read about it in a book my mom bought called *Who's in Charge?* It's by Dianne Wimsworth, who's supposed to be the world's greatest parent. She writes tips on how to make your kids turn out to be responsible and stay out of trouble. I read parts of the book, just to see what Mom might do to improve me. (Dad never reads it. He just listens to Mom talk about how brilliant Dianne Wimsworth is and goes "That's a generalization" or "I beg to differ.")

Before everything happened that turned me into an atheist, our family was normal, except for my dad's ponytail, which Mom wants to cut off. She liked it fifteen years ago when he was touring all over in a band – the Blind Boas. But he's worked at City Hall for twelve years now so she told him he needs a makeover; said she might send his picture to one of those makeover-type TV shows. "Ha ha," he said. "Very amusing."

Mom should talk. She could use a makeover too. She actually wears leggings. In public. But not plain ones. Ones with wild colors and shapes all over them. She bought them before I was even born! And she thinks it's cool to wear a purple-and-yellow toque with the earflaps flying, or a sundress with huge, bright gaudy flowers everywhere. She never leaves the house without her lips painted hot pink. So she sticks out, compared to most moms who usually wear regular clothes – nice pants, pastel shirts. They look normal, whether they stay home or go to an office.

My mom'd like to go to an office, preferably at the university, to teach art history. She actually does this already, but she only has one class. She says that's because there are too many men professors, and so she belongs to a committee that complains about it. When the women meet at our house it's very intense. I hear things like "old boys' club" and "same old, same old" and "national statistics." I used to think that if Mom could be a regular professor, she'd gradually become more normal. But that doesn't really matter anymore.

The point is, aside from my parents' small weirdnesses, we were once quite a normal family. And even though Dianne Wimsworth says it's important to encourage your child's uniqueness, I beg to differ. I was especially normal. Pretty much, anyway, which was what I especially liked about me. If a person doesn't want to be unique, that should be allowed. Nobody should tell her it's better to be different. Some kids just want to blend in. Now, if you're a major singing superstar, then okay, you couldn't very well be normal, could you? But, you'd get to choose to be Selena Gomez or Justin Bieber. No one forces *them* to be abnormal. But to have someone else, or *something* else, like God (maybe) decide for you that you won't be like everyone else…That. Just. Sucks.

Chapter 2

Last year, in grade seven, we studied the word *ironic*. When two things that are sort of opposite happen close together, you say it's ironic. Here's an excellent example: No sooner had I decided to become an atheist (for the second time), than my parents decided to send me to Camp Outlook – a *church* camp. How *IRONIC*.

I was sent there because they were "overwhelmed with life." I'd also done something extremely stupid and illegal, so they were treating me like a delinquent. While my behavior didn't help their situation, I wasn't the major stress. They were so totally thinking of themselves, I could *not* believe it.

They did the exact opposite of what Dianne Wimsworth said to do in times of "family crises." She said, and I quote: "Family crises should be seen as opportunities to teach children about what they can expect in their own futures. They should learn how to cope with difficult events."

She did *not* say "Send your kid to camp."

My parents told me they were sorry. What was best for *them* was to have a couple of weeks on their own to adjust to our "new normal," a stupid phrase considering how *ab*-normal we'd so obviously become.

"But why a *church* camp," I blurted, "when I don't even believe in God?"

Admitting it was my last resort.

They believe in God, so I expected a big stink, but it was like I'd said "Please pass the peas." They sat there in Mom's hospital room, like blobs, faces droopy and pale, the same way they'd been all week. Dad sighed deeply. "Shan, we've no energy to argue. On Sunday you go."

That's how I ended up in the backseat of the Gormleys' car on a pukingly hot August afternoon. Next to me was Mandy Gormley, my now former best friend. It'd been her mother's bright idea to take me to camp. When she heard about our terrible crisis, she insisted; said I'd love it because Mandy did. Puh-*lease*.

Dad stuck his head in the back window and quietly told me to stop scowling. Once we were on our way, I performed an excellent, arms-crossed, stare-out-the-window scowl for a long time. If we'd been allowed to take our iPods, I would have stuck my earbuds in for the whole trip. Instead, I just had to pretend not to hear any of Mrs. Gormley's questions. And I didn't say a word to Mandy for three good reasons:

1) she was an accomplice in my kidnapping;

2) when I asked her to promise not to tell anyone about my new abnormal family, and why I was being sent to camp, she'd said "okay" but not in a sincere way;

3) she was someone who'd recently made a major "error in judgment" regarding someone getting beat up, which was really making me wonder about her as a friend.

So Mandy and her mom chattered on like I wasn't even there. Then they tried again to break my powerful silence.

"Well Shan," began Mrs. Gormley, "have you brushed up on your campfire songs?"

"You're gonna l-o-o-o-o-ve the sing-alongs," Mandy chimed in, flipping her long hair. "They're so awesome. And with your voice, I bet they'll get you to lead!"

They were totally sucking up to me, but no way

was I getting excited. How could I be as excited as them anyway? For the first time they were going to camp not just for *one* week, but for *two*. Mrs. Gormley had always volunteered in the kitchen, but this year some other volunteer had cancelled for the following week, so Mandy's mom was filling in for her.

Mandy launched into a boisterous version of "Flying Purple People Eater," and Mrs. Gormley joined in. She wore a goofy sunhat covered with a zillion pins that rattled when she moved. (Mandy once told me she's addicted to buying them. She's probably spent a thousand bucks. *A thousand bucks!*)

Mandy punched my arm, tried to get me to join in, but I slouched down and got all the way to Outlook without singing a note. Past the town, we turned off the highway onto a gravel road. More trees and brush appeared on the open prairie, and camp signs sprang up.

"I know it's hard for you, dear," said Mrs. Gormley, "but you'll see. It'll be just what you need. Right, Mandy?"

"Right, Mom."

That's what was bugging me to pieces. Everyone knew what *I* needed. They were sitting there looking *sooooo* happy, *sooooo* thrilled. And why not? For them, everything was exactly the same. They were going along as usual in their oh-so-perfect world. They were going off to camp feeling completely normal. They'd *be* completely normal. It'd be super-easy for them to do all the churchy things and act like God loved everybody. Easy, easy, easy. *Their* absolutely fabulous, perfectly normal lives hadn't been changed *forever*.

And still, *they* knew what *I* needed.

They didn't have a clue.

Chapter 3

There was only one small problem with deciding to be an atheist, and this is something I've never told anybody, ever.

You see, when I was five years old I had a dream. In my mind's eye I saw a trillion multi-colored speckles of light. They swirled all around me and everything felt bright and happy. I felt loved, actually. Somehow deep, deep down, I knew that I was really looking at the soul of Jesus. The feeling was so intense that it woke me up and I've thought of it many times since. After eight years I still remember it clearly, so it must have been something important.

The problem? I was so sure Jesus had visited, but if I was now an atheist then there was no God so there couldn't be a Son of God and my dream could no longer mean anything. It was what it was: a bunch of colored speckles. The Jesus part was just something a five-year-old brain would add.

After what happened at camp, I still believe it was my own brain making up Jesus, but I'm not so one-hundred-percent-sure that the speckles were just speckles. As I see it, lots of strange things happen in this world that you can't explain. For starters, what about that incredible magician on TV? He's just like you and me, but he can float off the ground just out on a street with no rigged-up stage. If he floated in front of me, I'd definitely think there was something about this world I didn't understand.

And then there's the Ouija board. You put your fingers on this indicator-thingy and it moves around on a board that has the alphabet written on it and spells out answers to questions. The thingy moves all by itself. Mandy and I have asked a zillion questions and lots were answered right! (My dad said we're cuckoo for believing in a Ouija board, but then Mom said she used to get her tarot cards read, and it didn't do her any harm.)

And then there's church. Now there you have a

whole bunch of regular, smart people who believe Jesus rose up from the dead and walked around chatting to folks like he'd never been crucified. And when he was alive (the first time, not the second), he walked on water and performed lots of other miracles. My parents actually make me go to church, and I don't see my dad telling those people that they're cuckoo.

And one of their best friends is a normal-looking author who told us she used to write her books in an old building near Fort Qu'Appelle (which, by the way, was named for a First Nations legend about a ghost!), and it used to be a TB hospital where a lot of people died, but then it got turned into a retreat place and she told us that lots of her writer-friends have gone there and seen ghosts, and eventually she saw one too, so how do you explain that I'd like to know!!!

So if somebody doesn't believe me about Camp Outlook and they think I'm crazy, well then just too bad for them. It's pretty obvious to me when you get right down to it, that a lot of people you might think of as normal are actually pretty *ab*normal in their own certain particular ways.

Chapter 4

Mandy tugged on my T-shirt. "C'mon! Mom's gonna register us, so I can show you around."

I could feel what was about to happen. Mandy was going to drag me all over, telling me everything she already knew about Camp Outlook that I didn't. Typical.

She grabbed my hand and pulled me along a short road that led into a clearing.

"This is the Bowl," she announced, like a tour guide. We were standing in the middle of a large circle of cabins, a dozen of them, each a different color with a big open porch. They poked out from an even larger circle of shrubs and tall poplar trees. Their leaves shimmered like sequins in the sun. Everywhere, girls lugged backpacks and sleeping bags, and screen doors slammed in an off-beat rhythm.

"Sweet, eh?" she gushed. It was like a fairy tale, but I didn't let on. "I've stayed in the turquoise cabin, and in the yellow one twice. And last year I was in that green one, where that girl had the asthma attack I told you about."

Mandy'd told the story many times, and now, there was the very porch where the girl had almost died. Cool.

At each end of the Bowl was a large building. Mandy pulled me along to one that had a roof curving up to the sky, topped with a cross.

"This is the Gathering Hall. We do crafts here." The doorframe was wide and carved with intricate designs. Before I knew it I was showing more interest than I wanted to. I said, "Is that other building carved like this?"

"Nah, it's just the Mess Hall," she replied, "where you eat."

"I know what a Mess Hall is, Mandy. Jeesh." See, this makes me crazy, the way she assumes I'm stupid. It was probably a good thing we didn't share a cabin; I would've strangled her in her sleep. Luckily I was in the blue one, she was in yellow.

Blue got Sam, the coolest counselor by far. (At least that's what I first thought, until she made some *errors in judgment* later on.) She'd come all the way from Texas to spend the summer with her aunt. The aunt thought Sam should be a counselor for a few weeks.

Me and eleven other girls – my cabinmates – gathered at the blue porch steps. Everyone was either going into grade seven or grade eight, like me. Sam yelled, "So, who are ya'll?" and we stifled a giggle; her accent was hilarious. The girls began saying their names, where they were from, and so on. It occurred to me that Sam looked like Britney Spears. There was a butterfly tattoo on her ankle and a bellybutton ring poked out from under her low-cut tank top. Her top was so tight you could see her bra right through it, and she had the most cleavage I'd ever seen on a teenager. I was so busy wondering if Sam would get into deep doo-doo for her clothes that I totally didn't hear her say "And you?" Laughter brought me back to the question, which had been directed at me, and I answered like a dipstick because I wasn't thinking about what I was saying. I was thinking, *Did they see me staring at her boobs?* I wanted to hide under a rock. As the last girl introduced herself, all I could hear was every drop of blood whooshing into my cheeks. I felt woozy. I put my head down on my knees.

I hated this. I hated Mandy and her mom. I hated my parents. I hated my life. I hated me for hating my life.

Yeah, most of all, I hated me.

Chapter 5

And one last final thing that I showed my parents to prove I didn't need church camp.

Dianne Wimsworth, page 179:
Chapter 12: God and the Intelligent Child
It's entirely possible to bring up a moral child without benefit of religion or a belief in God. That said, religion is integral to the lives of many American families and can have both positive and negative influences upon our children. In this chapter we'll explore the challenges of raising a child in an atheistic home and a religious home. As a psychologist

I'm primarily interested in how atheistic parents handle what some call the "natural mysticism" of children, and conversely, how religious parents deal with a child's developing intelligence and his/ her capacity for doubt....

Anyway, it goes on and on, but you see? She clearly states: *It is entirely possible to bring up a moral child without benefit of religion or a belief in God.*

Nuff said.

Chapter 6

During vespers I was still seething with hatred about everything having to do with Camp Outlook. All the campers were sitting on a hill overlooking the river. A counselor was going on at us about living with "an attitude of gratitude" and being thankful for the beauty of the sunset before us. Blah, blah, blah. I rolled my eyes.

After the final prayer, which was all about having a nice week together, we followed a well-worn path to the campfire. We looked like crazed lunatics flapping our hands at the huge clouds of fish flies. Birds exploded from the brush when they heard us coming. I ran ahead to catch up with Mandy, who had a blanket over her arm. She asked if I liked my cabinmates.

"Sure," I said, even though I hadn't talked to them much. "They're okay. Have you seen our counselor? She's from Texas."

"How could I not see her?" Mandy said, and karate chopped a bug cloud. "She thinks she's a movie star."

"Does not," I argued. "She's actually really nice."

"Well, I bet she gets told to wear different clothes."

We walked on silently amid the chatter. Mrs. Gormley's voice pierced through, yelling to someone that whoever was supposed to be leading the sing-along was running late. The smell of the campfire was getting stronger.

"My cabin's pretty good," Mandy said. But she hesitated, then leaned in to whisper, "Actually, there's one super-snobby girl who's got super-long nails and her mom pays for her to get them manicured and painted with little flowers and jewels."

"Really?" I said with my usual Mandy-that's-amazing tone. *Why did I keep doing that?*

"And," she went on, even closer to my ear, "we've got this weird girl." She pointed. "You can see her over there. The one pulling off her sunglasses and rolling her head around."

She was taller than most of us, with thick, dark hair,

cut short. Even though it was nearly dark, she wore sunglasses that had shields to keep the sun out completely. Mandy linked her arm through mine and whispered, "There've been special needs kids here before, but she's *extra*-special. She's fifteen. Tanya – that's our counselor – Tanya says she's on the autism spectrum, whatever that means."

"It means there are different kinds," I was happy to explain.

Mandy shrugged. "Whatever. She's got some other strange problem, too. Tanya says we have to treat her the same as everyone else. But this girl either doesn't answer you, or she babbles nonsense. Snobbypants said it's going to wreck camp for all of us."

At least it was this Snobbypants person and not Mandy who thought that. I had to give her some credit there. I'm sorry to say that at the time, I was glad the weird girl wasn't in my cabin.

The path narrowed, so everyone slowed down to squeeze through an opening to where a huge fire was burning.

"Sit three circles deep around the fire pit please!" barked a counselor. Mandy and I sat on the outside circle with her blanket over our legs. It had been so hot earlier, but here beside the river, it was surprisingly cool. The autistic girl sat nearby, rocking and cooing. No one sat next to her until Tanya shuffled her bum over and put an arm around her.

"Your attention please, campers!" bellowed Poobah. She was in charge of everything, so she wore a T-shirt that said GRAND POOBAH, hence the nickname. "Campers! We lined up a great singer to lead us, but he's late, so you're stuck with me!" A big groan. A chortle from Poobah, then "A-one and a-two and *I wish I was a little bar of soap, oh I wish I was a little bar of soap…*"

They all jumped in. I knew the song, but not the two that followed it. Didn't matter. I refused to sing any of them – part of my ongoing protest. I wouldn't be sucked into any fun, not in front of Mandy or her mom, anyway.

Was it loud or what? A hundred singers drowned out the evening songbirds and crickets. I lay back, watched the smoke escape to the stars through a gap in the trees. Then, right in the middle of "Edelweiss," voices gradually dropped away and giggles erupted. Mandy whacked me and I sat up. Through the flames, on the other side of the fire, was a long-haired guy with a beard. He wore this blousy, cotton tunic-y thing and smiled broadly. Perfect white teeth sparkled in the firelight.

Mandy's mouth was at my ear saying, "Wow, I had

no idea Jesus was coming." I thought we'd burst a gut. He did look exactly like those Jesus paintings, which is what everyone else must've thought too, because within a day we were all calling him Jesus. Not to his face, of course.

"Bra-a-a-a-d!" Poobah exclaimed. "We were just getting warmed up."

"You sound fantastic," he said sincerely. "You don't need me!"

The teenage counselors were the first to disagree. Loudly. Then everyone else chimed in.

"Ladies! LADIES!" Poobah yelled, until we all shut up. "He's staying. He's on our payroll, after all." She winked at him. "Brad Stephenson is a theology student and in another couple of years he'll be a minister. He's working with two rural churches all summer, and they're loaning him to us. This is his fifth week of singing six nights a week!" Huge applause. "Now, where's your guitar?"

"Right here!" He turned. It'd been hanging down his back. One fancy rock star move and it magically appeared in his hands. He blasted some chords and sang, "All God's Critters Got a Place in the Choir..." Everyone sang but me.

Then something came over me. I wanted to be him.

He was so, *soooooo* cool. His voice was *soooooo* beautiful. He knew all sorts of funny tunes and used hilarious cartoon-y voices, which made it a lot harder for me to stay stone-faced. And he was *soooooo* nice. He said anyone could lead a song, even borrow his guitar. In my head I practiced "Bye, Bye Love," the way Dad had taught me.

I couldn't help it. I began to smile.

Chapter 7

I was conceived on my parents' honeymoon in Banff in the usual way. (Nuff said.) They were in Banff because the Blind Boas had been booked much earlier at one of the chalets, so it was convenient to have the wedding and honeymoon there the week before Dad had to work. I was a genuine surprise wedding gift. If I hadn't come along when I did, exactly nine months later, I'm sure Dad could've recorded his songs and become famous. And he could've made a music video because he's very good-looking. At least that's what my girlfriends say. (Once, Mandy even called him a "hottie." This is pukingly creepy coming from a friend.)

When I asked Dad if my being born wrecked his music career he said, "That was all your mom's doing," and winked at her. He was pushing her buttons, which he does to amuse himself and people other than my mom. "Not my fault you couldn't get enough of these," she replied, pointing to her hot-pink lips. There was a time when this kind of thing made me have to fake a big barf. Now I just roll my eyes, which is more mature.

Because I have my parents' genes, I inherited a couple of things that make me stick out a bit. From my dad I got my voice. I can sing pretty well. Not to brag, but people have told me so. I've done solos in school musicals. Dad taught me to play guitar, which I love, and downloading music is way cool. Last year I decided I wanted to be a singer. For a living, I mean. But Dad warned me it'd be a tough way to make a buck, which is why he's got a job-job now. (He calls music a job, but his city work is a job-job.) In any case, with my new family responsibilities, I've been thinking I will probably need a job-job.

Oh, that's from my mom: the responsibility gene. She's pretty much responsible for everything in the world. She complains to Dad and me, "Why must I be responsible for this?" or "Will someone please take responsibility for that?" or "Just what would you two do if I keeled over and died, hmm?" She plasters up sticky notes everywhere like a mad woman, lists of things she's no longer taking responsibility for, which makes me supremely annoyed because I do take responsibility for things. Maybe not just exactly when she wants.

Back when I was nine, after one of her sticky-note fits, I told her to stop getting on my case. It wasn't my fault there was only one of me.

"Maybe if I had a sister or brother all your stupid chores would be done!" I screamed at her. "Other moms have more than one personal slave!"

She glared at me for a moment, her eyes becoming wet and fierce. She yelled something, but her voice was warbley, and I couldn't understand her. I'd never seen her cry like that, bent over in two, just wailing. I was terrified she'd keel over and die, just like she'd threatened. She reached for the kitchen counter to help her keep upright, put her head down on her crossed arms, and bawled like I wasn't even there. Clueless, I put my arm around her.

"It's not your fault, Shan," she wept. "I'm just having a bad day. A very bad day."

I went up to my room and cried some myself. Even at age nine I knew deep down this wasn't good, and as it turned out, it was the very, very beginning of how I ended up at Camp Outlook.

For the next two years we would still seem like a regular family to others, but that was only because they couldn't see my mom sitting straight through a whole morning, staring out the window, a cold cup of coffee in her hands. And they never heard the floorboards creaking in the middle of the night, her creeping downstairs, a sob, a gasp, floating up the stairwell.

Chapter 8

The first night my cabinmates tittered until long after lights-out. Sam finally said they'd lose Tuck Shop privileges if they didn't shut up and sleep. I turned in my sleeping bag, the bunk springs squeaking in the silence. A few beams leaked in from the floodlight in the Bowl.

For the billionth time I thought about how sad my mom had been a few years earlier, the months and months she couldn't make herself do *anything*, never mind living with a stupid "attitude of gratitude." And now, after everything that had just happened, I wondered if she'd be sad for the whole rest of her life.

I yearned to be with her. Was she home yet? Or still

in hospital? How was Dad managing? Soon I was angry again, which meant it took me a long time to fall asleep. When the morning bell rang, it seemed I hadn't slept at all. I listened to everyone get up, until Sam gave me a poke.

"Hey sleepyhead, time for morning songs! I'm not supposed to leave anyone behind." I pretended to be dead, refused to cooperate. When they'd gone I dressed to the sound of a hundred voices singing "Morning Has Broken." Then Poobah shouted the words to an unfamiliar song, and the campers repeated it.

By the time I joined them, they were filing into the Mess Hall, and I was at the end of the line. All around me they babbled non-stop, clusters breaking into spontaneous song. I rolled my eyes and sighed deeply.

Inside, I grabbed a tray and dishes. "Shannon!" It was Mrs. Gormley, reaching out with a huge spoonful of gooey porridge. She plopped it into my bowl. "How was your first night?"

"Fine, thank you." I did not mention I was planning to run away. How would she like that? I poured milk on my cereal.

"You know, Shannon, your folks said to call anytime. You can use my cell."

"No, thank you. They're too busy to think about me."

"Shannon, you don't believe that's true."

I picked up some toast and slid my tray along, pretending not to hear her in the din.

All the benches were packed, except for the end of one row, right next to the weird girl from Mandy's cabin. I looked away from her, searching desperately for another place, but when I looked back I could tell she had seen me trying to avoid her. Even with her sunglasses on, hurt radiated from her face. My chest tightened with guilt.

"Hi," I said, more to her cabinmates than to her. "Okay if I join you?"

"Sure," they said, and went quiet as I sat down. Everyone was looking at me, and I wondered if Mandy had already blabbed about my situation. She waved from down the table and then the yakking picked up again. The girl next to her had fancy fingernails and turned away from me. Ah, yes. Miss Snobbypants. I focused on my porridge.

"Hey, what's your name?" The weird girl's breath wisped across my right cheek. I turned to find her face an inch from mine, which creeped me out.

"Shannon," I half-whispered.

"Which cabin?" She lifted her sunglasses. Her eyes were huge and brown, but one looked like milk had been poured over it.

"Blue."

"Blue," she repeated. "Blue."

She took another bite of toast, chewed and swallowed thoughtfully. "Blue, blue, bloob, belly," she began. "Bolly, billy, bobby, baby, boobie, boppee, blue, blue, blue." I looked to the other girls for help, but they were busy, or pretending to be. "Blue, right?"

"Yes," I said.

"Shannon, right?"

"Yep."

"Shannon, banon, canon, lanon, panon, fanon, Shannon, Shannon, Shannon." She got louder and still everyone ignored her.

"Me," she went on, "I'm stonnie. Stonnie, wonnie, jonnie, fonnie, lonnie, ronnie, onnie, onnie, onnie. Okay, wanna know my name?"

I nodded.

"Bonnie."

"Nice name," I said. Toast caught in my throat.

"Means sweet and beautiful. Sweet, beet, wheat, meat, creet, deat, sheet, eat, feet, jeet, neat, queet, veet, seat, eeeeeeeeeeet!"

I needed to get away from her, but just as I stood she lifted her sunglasses again, looked at me sadly and said, "You're pretty." A terrible whoosh went through me. I knew I was being mean to her. I wasn't trying to be, it was just coming out of me as if it had a mind of its own. I sat down again.

"Thanks, Bonnie. That's nice of you."

She beamed, and then lowered her glasses.

"Too bad you have to wear those," I told her. "You have very big eyes."

"Beautiful eyes?"

"Sure," I replied. After all, her left eye was perfect.

"Beautiful, beautiful," she repeated with a giggle. "Beautiful, bute, bute, boot, bobble, buggle, butt, borp." She babbled on as she stood up. "Borble, bibble, baba, bib, baba, bib," and then, just as she was leaving the table, I swear I heard her say, "Bute, bute, beautiful, beautiful, beautiful, baby, baby, baby, Gabriel."

My heart stopped.

"What? What did you say?" I shouted after her as she headed to the kitchen to return her tray. Heads turned. By the time I'd thought to follow her she was at the door, but a counselor turned me back to clean up my dishes. Once I'd finally dropped my tray on the trolley, Bonnie was gone.

I found her sitting on the front steps of the yellow cabin. Her glasses were off and she was staring at the sun, sticking her tongue in and out.

"Bonnie," I gasped, "what did you say back there?"

She looked at me blankly.

"At the table. You know, baby, baby, baby…?"

A broad smile brightened her face as she said, "Hey, what's your name?"

"It's Shannon. Remember?"

She laughed like it was the funniest thing she'd ever heard and never spoke to me again.

Chapter 9

If I had a big important secret the one person I would never, ever, *ever* tell is Mandy Gormley. Here's why.

Last year, in grade seven, a new kid came to our school, just for grade eight. His name was Al Warner. My cousin, who goes to another school, told me Al had been in his class, but he punched a teacher in the face and got kicked out forever. I told Mandy this and swore her to secrecy. But with her, she'd die if she didn't tell somebody. So she went and told an eighth-grader, Sue Morrison, who Mandy wanted to be friends with because Sue had recently become one of the Cools.

A couple days later, Al Warner caught me at recess,

thumped me up against the sharp bricks of the school, and used a lot of swearing to explain it had been very stupid of me to tell anyone what he'd done to that teacher. He didn't punch me, but he left me shaking, and you can bet I told off that Mandy. She blamed Sue, but wouldn't tell her off because she wanted to stay buddy-buddy with her.

And another thing: Mandy gets way excited when she knows something you don't, like when Rod Goldman got in deep doo-doo for drinking beer by the skating rink – he's only thirteen! – or when Elsa Miner's oldest sister, Donna, had a premature baby and nobody, not even Donna herself, knew it was coming. Mandy loves to tell you these things and you have to sit there, amazed.

Mandy's grade-eleven sister tells her a lot of juicy information. "Did you hear, Shan?" Mandy'll begin, even though she knows I'm an only child and never hear anything. "Scott Walker dumped Rebecca Day and right away he hooked up with Erin Tootoosis!"

The problem is I *am* interested. I mean, Erin Tootoosis? How's a person supposed to hide her shock and amazement about something like that? Scott's grade eleven. Erin's grade eight!

There's still a lot Mandy doesn't know, and that's when she'll pull out her Ouija board. (It was actually her mom's when she was a kid. Mrs. Gormley is a true pack rat.) The board is painted with the alphabet and numbers zero to nine. On the left side is a YES, on the right side a NO.

We first started using it in grade six. Mandy and I would sit cross-legged on the floor, facing one another, the board balanced on our legs. We'd set our fingers on the pointed indicator-thingy, super-lightly. We'd close our eyes and Mandy'd begin with a test question, "Oh, great Ouija spirit…what's the name of our dog?" and the indicator would slide miraculously to the letters spelling POOCHY. Amazing.

"Oh, great Ouija spirit," she'd go on, "does Doug (or Jake or Colin or Mick or Shayne) like me?"

The indicator would stutter across to YES and Mandy'd squeal. "When will he tell me?" And it'd spell out the date.

It's lame that we mostly asked about boys, but we really needed to know if we were ever going to have boyfriends before we graduated from eighth grade. Starting high school with zero boy experience would be intensely horrible. (Mandy said she'd make up a boyfriend if she had to; a "summer fling" is what her sister called it. No one knows it didn't actually happen because you had it when you were away on your holidays.)

One day she said, "So Shannon, you gonna ask about Rick?" I'd told her I'd caught him staring at me in the library. We placed our fingertips and breathed deeply.

"Oh, great Ouija spirit, will I ever be Rick Santana's girlfriend?"

We waited, eyes closed. Something delicious wafted under the bedroom door. I heard someone entering the house. The indicator moved, only slightly, towards NO, then backtracked to YES. We screamed, fell over, laughing ourselves silly at our ridiculous squeals. As we caught our breath, I heard Mrs. Gormley laughing over the muffled voice of Mandy's dad. Then he guffawed real loud. It had been a long time since I'd heard my parents laugh like that. In fact, that morning my mom had had one of her "episodes" when for no reason at all, she burst into tears.

I bolted upright and grabbed the board. Mandy reached for the indicator and I pulled it away from her. "I have to ask this one by myself."

She looked hurt. "About Ricky-poo?"

"No." I closed my eyes and focused. When I'd been quiet for too long she said, "Aren't you going to ask?"

"Not out loud." I was a little pleased to see she was annoyed. I shut my eyes again. *Oh, great Ouija spirit, will my family ever be normal again?*

Plates clattered in the kitchen. Mrs. Gormley shouted, "Mandy! Send Shannon home and wash up!" I squeezed my lids tight. A surge of energy passed through my hands. I stared down at the metallic mauve of my fingernails and watched the indicator slide. Without hesitating, it moved straight to NO.

Chapter 10

One thing was for sure: I would not be telling Mandy about what I thought I heard Bonnie say. *Baby Gabriel.* What if Mandy told others – made it sound like I was the loony one? I couldn't risk looking any more abnormal than I already was.

In this world there are different kinds of abnormal. Some abnormals you can't see because they're private, like in my family. Then there are abnormals everyone sees, like if you're too smart or too quiet or too fat or too skinny or too poor or speak funny or have freckles or wear the wrong clothes or wear braces or a bra too young or play classical music or read too much or you're bad at sports or you laugh weird or you've got strange relatives or you're a good singer or you bring gross food for lunch or any of about a thousand other things. And then there's the kind of abnormal no one would dare pick on you for, an abnormal so major you'd never get teased because it'd be so obviously cruel. That would be an abnormal like Bonnie.

These things went through my head as I sat at the back of the Gathering Hall, watching her tie on an apron. How had she known Gabriel's name? Mandy assured me she hadn't mentioned him to her cabinmates, but I couldn't be certain.

Bonnie was sitting alone, and that made me think of Bruce Kordinski, the only person in my school who was intellectually disabled and was in a wheelchair. Kids avoided him, including me. We didn't know what to say to him because he couldn't talk. He'd be going into grade four. His older brother, Paul, was a grade behind me and always looked out for Bruce. He was quiet and responsible and also considered geeky. For a moment I remembered Paul's face, covered in blood. I focused harder on what was going on around me, pushed the image out of my brain.

Half the campers were here, and the rest had gone swimming. I'd fibbed to Sam, saying I felt sick, thinking

I'd get to stay in the cabin. She said we weren't allowed to be there unsupervised, so here I sat, next to the door, in case I needed to throw up, she said.

Poobah, in shorts and an orange chef's apron that said GRAND POOBAH, blew her whistle. Three ladies my mom's age joined her, wearing matching orange aprons with their names on them.

"Girls! Meet our talented Craft Team. You'll love what they've planned for the week." I rolled my eyes.

"Nicole, Karen, and Lori are all award-winning artists and they'll be here for two weeks. Nicole is a quilting champ. Karen weaves and just had a piece selected for a national show, and Lori is a painter. She sells her work all over the world through her website. They've all set up their studios in the rooms off the hall, and you can visit them anytime."

Applause broke out and the three women laughed, especially Lori, who bowed, and came up smiling like she'd swallowed the sun. They began to demonstrate how to make a pair of praying hands out of plaster, using a mold. I was sorry to be fake-sick because it looked like fun. Lori showed us how she'd painted three sets of hands, two like skin, and one sprayed gold. They were beautiful. Nicole said we'd have to let the plaster dry and then paint them tomorrow.

Soon everyone was in line for supplies, then busy with mixing and pouring. A few girls looked over at me, pointed and whispered, probably wondering why I was just sitting there. The craft ladies moved from table to table giving more instructions, and telling the loudest girls to keep it down. There was white powder and gobs of plaster everywhere.

Sam, who wore the shortest T-shirt and lowest low-waist pants I'd ever seen, was too busy helping my cabinmates to be bothered checking on me, so I crossed my arms and leaned back in my chair with my eyes closed. I imagined running away. Now would be the perfect time – just run to the cabin for my things, take the bush path to the parking lot, and hide until a car arrived. Maybe it'd be Jesus' car! The night before he'd walked back with us, said he'd be driving over from Outlook every night. From there I could get a bus ticket to Saskatoon with my tuck money. I'd just wait till he left his car, then hide in the back. He'd return from campfire, drive us to his house. Magically there'd be another campfire burning in his backyard – he'd sit there with his guitar singing "Kumbaya" while I snuck from his car to hide in a nearby bush. It would be just him and me under the stars and then...

"Shannon!"

My eyes snapped wide open and there, with its nose pressed on mine, was a Cyclops! I leapt from my chair in terror, kicking the beast in its shin so hard it began hopping on one leg. It howled and the room went silent. I caught my breath, took a second look. My Cyclops was Lori, the painter. Poobah rushed over to help her. Sam ran to me. "What y'all doin' here?"

Lori recovered in no time and all eyes turned on me. My face was totally red for the second time since arriving.

"You okay?" asked Poobah.

"Fine. She was right in my face and scared me. It was an accident. I'm so sorry."

It seemed to me that Lori should also apologize, but instead she behaved like nothing weird had happened. She gave me a big smile and said slowly, "Come make hands. You and me."

Without waiting for my answer she grabbed my arm and yanked me over to the supply table. Everyone went back to whatever they'd been doing. Lori poured water into the plaster while I stirred and kept my head down, so she couldn't see I was crying.

"Pay 'tention," she said. "Gently. No bubbles."

The plaster got smoother.

"Here," she said, "take these." A couple of tissues were waving under my nose. I looked up and thanked her. She was the same height as me and for the first time I noticed her eyes. I wondered if she was part Chinese. And then I had the strange feeling that we already knew one another. There was something familiar, warm.

"How'd you know my name?"

She handed me another tissue.

"Shannon," she said, giving me one of her prize-winning smiles, "everything will be fine. Soon you will be part of the circle. You are blessed."

What? Blessed? To be a camper? She was a total loon. Without saying another word we poured the plaster into the mold. Then she surprised me with a huge hug before she left to help someone else.

"Glad you're feeling better," shouted Sam, who was cleaning up our cabin's table. "Soon as y'all are finished c'mon meet us at the Tuck Shop."

"Okay," I replied. As she threw one last batch of wet newspaper into the bin, she gave me a wink and a nod, like she thought I was an okay person, then left.

By the time my plaster had finally set, the hall was empty. I pushed in the wire hook and scratched my initials into the damp surface. Prying it from the mold, its cold surface shot a chill up my arms. I went to place it with the others and was about to set it down when I began feeling genuinely queasy, so I sat on the floor and swallowed hard several times. *Soon you'll be part of the circle.* I turned the form over in my hands, inspected the bony male fingers and perfectly filed nails. *You are blessed. You are blessed.* Lori's voice would not leave my head. I closed my eyes. *Everything's going to be fine.* Trembling, I opened my eyes and set my piece on the floor next to the long row of ghostly, severed hands, then ran back to my cabin as fast as my legs would carry me.

Chapter 11

Not to sound like a broken record, but I'm pretty close to normal. ("Not to sound like a broken record" is what Mom says to Dad when she's asked him too many times to do something. Today you should really say "Not to sound like a skipping CD.")

Except for the minor things I already mentioned, like having a good voice, I'm normal. When I was little, my mom tried to make me stick out and consequently we have pictures of me dressed in the stupidest things. She liked to shop at crafty-type festivals for "unique" clothes and once she even had me dressed to look like a black-and-white cow – with a tail! Thank goodness no one knew me back then, especially Rick Santana. I'd have to slit my wrists.

Sometimes normal kids are planned for and sometimes not. Even though I was a surprise, my parents said they loved me very much. But, loving me that much took a lot of time and energy, and Dad was still on the road, so they waited until I was in grade one before they started to try for another baby.

This was a big mistake. Dad should've stopped traveling sooner, and then they could've had a baby while I was little, and we'd have ended up a totally normal family.

Instead, two years and nine months ago, when I was in grade five, they left me with my cousins and went to Calgary. When they got back we had a long talk about how they weren't able to have another baby. Finally I knew why Mom cried so often and why Dad couldn't fix it. They said we'd be making more trips to Calgary because there was a hospital there where the doctors could help.

Back then, Mom was already thirty-nine, pretty old, and Dad was thirty-five. (I would have to live my life two more times over to catch up to them!) Since they'd produced me, their inner parts had deteriorated. They would need "technological intervention."

I was allowed to go on the next trip because it was still summer, just before grade six. Also, they had to be there for two whole weeks, so they pretended it was a holiday, and we stayed in a hotel with a pool. (Once I heard Dad complain that this would be our last holiday for a long time because the cost of baby-making was ridiculous.) Before we'd left home Mom had already started to get needles every day. *Every day!* Dad had to give them to her, which made me gag because I'm totally not a needle person. The needle-drug would help her produce lots of eggs.

The first night in our hotel room, Mom said she felt like "a bloody pin cushion" because she couldn't sit normal since she got all the needles in her butt and it "hurt like hell." That whole first week she was crabbier than usual, which I could tell by the number of times she swore.

One afternoon, Dad and I escaped to the zoo. (In Dianne Wimsworth's book this is called "removing yourself from the situation.") Looking at animals used to be the kind of thing Dad would get excited about. Actually, he used to get excited about a lot of things I liked to do. Mom always said he was really just a big kid at heart. When I was little, he'd been the one who actually enjoyed playing endlessly with my toys and me. But at the zoo it was easy to tell he didn't really want to be there.

"Are you worried about Mom?"

He smiled a little and shook his head. "Yep. A little."

"Why?"

"I'm worried she won't know when to stop doing this. And I'm thinking about what it's really gonna cost. And that I should probably be playing music on the weekends, which means more time away from you. I just don't know if we're doing the right thing."

"But Dad, we might have a baby."

"And we might not."

Every day the doctors looked at my mom's ovaries until finally, a week after we'd arrived, her eggs were ready to pop. That day her tummy had puffed up till it was rock-hard. She could barely walk for the pain, but she had to wait another whole day for the "harvest."

When the doctor finally operated inside her, he used a little vacuum to suck out thirty-four human eggs!!! The doctor said a woman my mom's age would usually produce only three or four eggs.

"How about that Shan," Dad said with a wink, "your mom's a genuine freak of nature."

"Oh, ha ha," Mom replied, but you could see she thought she was super-human. She was happy.

Two days later we got the good news that almost

twenty of the fertilized eggs had survived and were dividing properly. The doctor did what's called in vitro fertilization. He put five of them into her uterus and then froze all the leftovers.

Back at the hotel Mom rested on the bed, and Dad pulled an envelope out of his bag. "So Shan, ever wonder what you looked like when you were three days old?"

Inside the envelope was a large photo of five bubble clusters.

"The babies?"

Mom spoke without opening her eyes. "One might be, if it has the good sense to attach itself to my cosy little womb."

"Or two or three," said Dad with a nervous laugh.

"Not likely," she replied, the happiness gone from her voice.

"Or all five!" I shouted, imagining her the size of a beluga. Where would we store five babies in our puny house? Mom sighed heavily.

That night in bed I mentally listed who I'd tell. Mandy would be sixth, or else everyone would know before I got to tell them. I pictured the baby bubbles, wondered which would become my sibling, and I heard myself whisper, "Please, God. Please."

Chapter 12

Once I believed that if I just prayed hard enough, Mom would have a baby. That was when I still believed in God, back when what I learned at church made a little sense, and Jesus himself had appeared in a dream. Weren't my parents good people? They prayed, did church. Bad stuff happened to other people, of course, but you couldn't expect the whole world to be rosy.

At Camp Outlook you had to pray like crazy. Every meal, every sunrise, every sunset, every campfire. Jesus usually led vespers with his guitar and hymn-type songs. We'd have to say the Lord's Prayer together, so I protested by staring at him, hoping he'd open his eyes and ask why

I wasn't participating. Then I imagined telling him how God was NOT always loving and compassionate. How God doesn't answer your most important prayers. How praying to God was stupid. That believing in all that was a joke.

When I think back on camp there's still anger in my belly. It's no wonder I didn't make a lot of friends or have much fun that first week. But it wasn't just me. Part of it was the number of Cools in our cabin. It doesn't matter where you go – ballet classes, swimming lessons, science camp, school. If there are kids, it doesn't take long before everyone knows who the truly cool ones are. By the second day in our cabin, Sidney, Carri, Alison K., Maggie, and Kaitlin had taken over: the loudest, the funniest, the cutest, the most fashionable, the most athletic. They were instantly popular with most of the campers. Sidney and Carri were especially noticeable, making them *Ultra-cools*. They were mouthy with Sam, but sucked up to her too. They snuck in cigarettes, and I know because on my way to the outhouse late one night I ran into them. As they passed me in the dark, the glint of burning tips swung back and forth like fireflies at the end of their arms. How they never got caught is a mystery, but this is another thing about Cools: They *never* get caught.

On Tuesday, the third day, at Craft Time, Sidney

painted her plaster hands to look like they'd been freshly amputated and crudely stitched together in prayer. Naturally, half the campers had to copycat her. Before the Craft Team knew it, the hall had been turned into the Texas Chainsaw Massacre. Lori, who had shown us how to paint the hands beautifully, burst into tears. Some girls felt bad about that. But nobody in charge asked who started it. The other adults just rolled their eyes at the girls and pretended nothing was wrong. (They'd probably read Dianne Wimsworth's book where it says sometimes children are just trying to get attention, and that's when you shouldn't give it to them. I personally wanted Poobah to ground them.)

Three other girls from my cabin besides me did not copy Sidney. They were Alison H., Darlene, and Sheila. Dar and Sheila were First Nations and came from a reserve up north. Alison came from a town near the reserve, so she'd become friends with them. Together they weren't exactly cool, but they weren't dorky either. The Cools would talk to me sometimes, but these three made the effort to really include me. Unfortunately, I was a jerk. They'd say "Wanna come to the Tuck Shop?" and I'd say "No, I want to read." Then I'd go alone later. Or they'd say "Wanna come with us to vespers?" and I'd say "I'm not ready." I'm surprised anybody liked me at all.

Halfway through the week I missed Mandy, weird as it sounds. During the days we'd been on different schedules. At meals our cabins sat at opposite ends of the hall. We sat together at campfire, but then there wasn't much time to talk.

On Wednesday night at the fire pit, you could smell rain in the air. Mandy and I chose a spot close to the fire and pulled her blanket around us. Unfortunately, Jesus arrived after us, and he chose to stand at the farthest point away. As he pulled his guitar out of its case he yakked with the adoring girls at his feet. I vowed I would never again choose my spot before he did.

"Guess what?" Mandy said gleefully. "Poobah told your counselor to quit dressing so slutty."

"How would you know?"

"She was at our cabin crying on the porch, telling Tanya all about it. She's really angry; wants to go back to Texas."

My stomach tightened and I looked for Sam. She was in the back row, a few yards over, wearing a baggy sweatshirt and looking glum. Now I knew why she'd been so snarky all afternoon.

Dar, Sheila, and Ali were the last to arrive and without thinking I waved them over. It surprised me as much as them.

"Wanna share our blanket?" I offered, forgetting it was Mandy's, but she didn't mind. We all sat real close as Jesus bashed out a few chords. "Okay campers – anybody know 'The Little Blue Man?'" Only a few put up their hands, so he played around, making us sing two lines at a time, over and over. Then he made us mimic his goofy voices till it all fell apart with the laughing.

"He's, like, so totally hilarious," said Mandy, zipping up her windbreaker. "Whoever heard of a hilarious minister? And he's a genuine hottie. Our whole cabin says so. Are hotties allowed to be ministers?" She wasn't really asking me, she was just babbling. "I mean, is it Christian to be a hottie? Then I told them they shouldn't call him Jesus anymore – it was kind of sick because the real Jesus wasn't a hottie. I don't think it said so in the…"

"For crying out loud Mandy," I hissed, "will you shut up pleeeease! I can't hear him."

"Well, *sorreeeee*."

I'd missed the chorus of a new song now. *Jeesh*. I stumbled along, watching his mouth. Then we sang "Boom! Boom! Ain't It Great to be Crazy?" and "Beans in my Ears" and a few others I already knew. After that he went over to Bonnie and sang "Sailing Over the Silly Sea" to her. She was huddled with Tanya under a blanket.

There's a repeated part where you shout "Hey, hey, hey!" Bonnie did it right every time. She looked pleased with herself.

Mandy leaned into my ear. "This afternoon Bonnie pinched Snobbypants and called her a meanie. Tanya told her off, so Bonnie refused to talk or leave the cabin. My mom had to stay with her so the rest of us could go swimming."

"Really?"

"Really."

Jesus began strolling through the crowd, playing "Four Strong Winds" and we five under the blanket bellowed it out. Dar leaned over to me and said, "You've got a great voice."

I grinned inside. "Thanks." Maybe camp wasn't so bad. This suddenly seemed like a good place to be, cuddled up with an old friend and some new ones, singing my heart out while staring at a guy who reminded me more and more of Rick Santana, if Rick could grow a beard. Life was *a little bit of okay*, as Dad would say. For the first time in ages I thought I should count my blessings, as my parents constantly reminded me to do.

I looked over at Bonnie. She seemed happy singing with everyone, being part of the group. Maybe she'd had a reason to pinch Snobbypants. What if she'd been mean to Bonnie first? Just then thunder cracked and the dark sky flashed silver.

"Campfire's over girls!" yelled Poobah, leaping to her feet. We'd barely got ourselves picked up when a mega-dump of rain landed on us. We pushed and squeezed through the small path out of the pit, then ran, but we were drenched long before we got to the Bowl.

It poured non-stop for two days, a natural disaster that some might call an act of God; the kind of thing that you can't control, that can wreck everything, even when you're at a church camp doing churchy things to serve God. How *ironic*. It was just one more reason to be suspicious about what God was up to, if you accepted that God existed at all.

Chapter 13

Dad says *an act of God* is just an expression. God is not behind every disaster on Earth. It's not like God is up in the sky planning everything out on a laptop. Dad says the idea of God is very complex, but he hasn't really explained what he means by that. He just says he doesn't agree with some church people about certain particular things. But he still goes there. And makes me go, too.

Back when I was almost eleven – just after we'd returned from Calgary and were waiting the two weeks to see if Mom's procedure had worked – I told Dad I was saying lots of prayers for Mom to get pregnant so we could be a normal, happy family again. The way I understood it, you were supposed to keep asking God and never give up hope. "Seek and ye shall find." That's what Jesus said. (The real one, not Brad.) I'd been staring at the photo of the five bubble-babies and asking God over and over to make one stick.

"So Shan, what'll you do if your prayers aren't answered?" Dad said.

"They will be," I assured him. Half his mouth smiled, but he didn't look me in the eyes.

I was super-positive for two reasons. First, Mom was so much her old self again. She was up and doing things around the house. There were sticky notes everywhere! I overheard her tell Dad that if there was going to be a baby in nine months, then this place needed to be straightened up, and he'd better get started on that list of jobs she'd given him last year. "Yes dear," he sighed, but I could hear the smile in his voice.

Second, I'd been at Mandy's playing Ouija. One of the private, silent questions I'd asked was whether or not any of the eggs would end up being my brother or sister. My heart almost burst when the immediate answer was YES.

Mandy wanted to know why I was so obviously excited, but I'd promised my parents to keep it a family secret for now. Besides, Mandy was way down The List of Who To Tell. It was driving her crazy that I could keep a secret, unlike herself.

"I thought we were best friends," she said in her effort to weasel it out of me. I was a tiny bit sorry then, but all I could say was "I can tell you soon, just not now."

"When?"

"In three months."

"Three months? That's forever!"

And she was right. It was forever. The Great Ouija had been wrong. And all my prayers had not worked. Not one freaking egg stuck. Fortunately, Mandy soon forgot about my secret, anyway. I never again asked the Ouija anything about babies.

Still, those first two weeks back from Calgary, between Mom's happiness and the Great Ouija, I so totally believed I would soon have a sibling. Like Mom, I'd been imagining baby things scattered all over the house. My friends would come over to hold our baby and I'd be more like a mom myself looking after it, not just a sister. I had just started a babysitting course so that when it came I'd know exactly what to do.

So the day I came home from school to find Dad back from work early, making tea, and Mom sitting at the kitchen table, eyes all red and puffy, my stomach lurched even before my brain thought *No baby*. I couldn't believe how much it hurt. They could see I knew what had happened, but Dad just said "Go take off your coat." But I didn't. I stood there holding my backpack. "It didn't work, did it."

Mom stared into her tea. Dad shook his head.

"So now what'll you do?"

"Like we said before," he replied, "we'll go back and try again. We've still got plenty of frozen eggs left; enough for at least three more tries."

And that's when all this stuff came pouring out of my mouth, things I'd no idea I even wanted to say. I began yelling at them. "And what if it never *ever* works? What if you can never have another baby ever again?" Mom cried even more. My dad gave me a hard look and said "We'll cross that bridge when we come to it."

"But I need to know now," I screamed, throwing my pack to the floor. "I need to know right now if you'll ever be happy again with just me. What if I can't make you happy again all by myself? What then?"

There was so much anger in me I hardly recognized myself.

Mom got off her chair and came to me, held me tight. I blubbered into her shoulder. "Oh Shannon," she went, "Shannon, my baby, I'm *so* sorry." She let go of my shaky body, kissed my forehead, and went up to bed.

Dad sighed heavily. "It'll be okay, Shan. One day. Really. Baby or not. It's hard for Mom to let go of the picture we'd had, for you and for us. You forget, at one time we'd even talked about wanting four kids."

I sniffled and nodded.

"And we kept all this from you for five years. Do you know how hard that was?"

I nodded again.

"And where'd you get the idea that families are happy all the time?"

"I didn't say we had to be happy *all* the time. But I'm sick of it being sad *most* of the time. Why can't I be enough for you?"

Dad sat down, reached for my hands and drew me to him. He spoke softly. "It's not about you. Between you and me, I think your mom's not just sad; she's depressed. She's not herself, not like the person I married. I haven't had the heart to suggest she get help. So please, go easy on her."

"Depressed?"

"It's worse than sad. You need to see a doctor about it."

My dad's eyes had gone watery. I didn't want to see him cry so I turned to leave. "We want this for you too, Shan. We know you'd be a fantastic sister."

I should've hugged him, but I was too choked up. In my room I closed the door, lay down on my bed, and when I began to hear Mom sobbing again through the wall, I put my pillow over my head and squeezed it.

I wish I could say that the next time they went to Calgary Mom came back truly and finally pregnant, that the sadness in our house ended. But that isn't what happened. And since I don't want it to sound like my whole life is one big, fat sob story, here's the super-short version of what did happen:

After the day I went ballistic on my parents, Mom treated me different. She tried harder. She did more with me and cried less. She got herself a second university class to teach so she was busier, without so much time to think about things.

As for Calgary, I never went again. When my parents went – which was for just a few days each time – I stayed at my uncle and aunt's twice, and once with Mandy. We told her family that my parents were away on business. A white lie that's allowed.

I changed a bit too, especially when things got to be the worst they could be. I gave Mom a lot more hugs and tried not to bug her or complain. Because, you see, she did eventually get pregnant, not once but twice. I was still in grade six. The first time it only lasted a month, but the second time it was almost three months, and we were just about to tell the world, when she lost our baby. I say "our baby" because of what Dad had said about me being a great sister. I wanted more than ever to be one, and the price was to be sad for a while longer. I cried hard about our lost babies, even though I had no idea who they would've been. It was strange to feel like you really loved somebody you hadn't even met, except in your imagination.

Mom and Dad tried to cheer me up by saying some embryos weren't healthy enough, and a miscarriage was nature's way of ensuring a healthy baby. They didn't listen to that themselves though because a few times I caught them crying together. They tried to pretend they weren't, but I could tell.

I'd seen kids cry lots, but what most kids don't know is adult sadness is completely and totally different. With a kid you just offer ice cream or something and it goes away. But with grown-ups it's like sadness has been tattooed onto their faces. They wear it all day and take it to bed at night. Dianne Wimsworth really ought to write a book for us kids about how to cope with parents. She acts like we cause the problems, but I mean, really, how's a kid in grade six supposed to know what to say to a grown-up who can't get out of bed for three days straight? Or what do you do when you're sitting in church, just going along like usual, and they start to have a baptism and the next thing you know your mom's sniffling and pulling out tissues, and you're too mortified to look at her because there you are, practically at the front where everyone can see that your mom's about to have a major breakdown? What's a kid supposed to do *then*? A little advice on *that* from Ms. Wimsworth would certainly be appreciated.

Chapter 14

For two days solid it rained and rained and rained.

Early Thursday morning Kaitlin, who was on a top bunk, awoke with a screech. The bottom of her sleeping bag was soaked. Our cabin, and a couple of others, were leaking.

We skipped the "Morning Has Broken" ritual; a small lake had formed in the middle of the Bowl. The water was cold, but a few campers ran through it for fun anyway. Everyone was in rain gear, which we'd been told to bring. Most of us had very bad hair, except Miss Snobbypants, who was the only one carrying an umbrella.

At breakfast Poobah shouted across the tables, "Ladies! Please and thank you! Swimming, hiking, and sports are cancelled, obviously, but that won't stop the fun. Lots of indoor activities are planned. Tomorrow is supposed to be First Nations Day, but if the rain continues we won't be raising the tepee. We'll still carry on with the other events. And remember, tonight it's a Backwards Dinner!"

"A what?" Ali asked to no one in particular.

Sheila stopped picking the raisins out of her porridge. "It's when everyone wears their clothes backwards, and walks backwards, and the meal starts with dessert."

"And ladies," Poobah went on, "vespers will be here right after supper and campfire's at the Gathering Hall. Some of the gravel roads are mud holes already, so if Brad doesn't make it, you'll be stuck with me."

There was a great groan, which made Poobah laugh. "I know. I feel exactly the same way!"

I checked my watch. Eight-thirty. Twelve hours to go before he might show up. There was a twinge in my chest.

Everything dragged. In the Gathering Hall we made macramé friendship bracelets and cool-looking crosses out of burnt wooden matchsticks. In between we jazzercised to ancient music only our moms would love. Later we had workshops. You could pick from wilderness survival (eating bugs and such like), astronomy (even though you wouldn't be able to find constellations that night, thanks to the clouds), and the one I chose: glamor makeup (taught by Sam and Tanya).

The two of them were dressed in non-camping clothes. Tanya, especially, didn't look like herself; more like Avril Lavigne when she first got famous (not like now), with big black eyes and straight streaked hair. Sam still looked Britney-fied, though her top was baggier, so now every time she bent over she practically flashed us. I couldn't help but wonder what Jesus thought of her. If I found her boobs hard to ignore, how hard would it be for a guy? He was going to be a minister, so he must have some kind of special non-typical-guy willpower.

Tanya's gear filled a shoebox, while Sam had brought a huge tackle box all the way from Texas. They'd prepared a major presentation and insisted we all take notes as if it was beauty school. Alison K. and Miss Snobbypants were their models. The best part was Sam's story about getting her belly button pierced. The worst part was when Bonnie – who was now like Tanya's shadow – kept helping herself to makeup, even though Tanya kept saying not to. The whole time Snobbypants was letting out big exasperated sighs, as if Bonnie was trying to annoy her and her alone. Finally, after Bonnie grabbed something for the billionth time, Snobbypants screamed, "Gaawd Bonnie, you are such an incredible idiot!"

We froze, waiting to see what Bonnie would do – what the counselors would do. Bonnie began weeping, so Tanya reached for her hand, then snapped at Snobbypants. "Christine, we've been over this. You need to learn patience."

Sam blew powder over Snobbypants' perfect face, and with her eyes closed she replied, "Right. Patience."

Time seemed to stand still during supper and vespers, but at long last it was eight-thirty and everyone was back at the Gathering Hall stripping off wet coats and boots. No sign of Jesus. In the darkened room, Poobah got us organized in our usual three circles around an amazingly realistic electric campfire. It cast a spooky glow on everyone's faces. Dar, Ali, Sheila, and I joined the inner circle. Someone shrieked, and we all looked over the fire to catch Lori holding Bonnie's hand. They were having a good belly laugh about something. Lori was still wearing a denim apron, covered with bright paint. Poobah's voice cut through the din.

"Ladies, as you can see, Brad hasn't arrived. Keep your fingers crossed he isn't stuck somewhere."

I crossed my fingers, arms, legs, and toes. Mandy

waved her crossed fingers at me from the other side of the circle. Poobah boomed the "Welcome Song," but she started too low, so we sounded like men. Just as we finished, the door swung open and yesssssss! There was Jesus! He came in singing, in the same low key, which you could hardly hear at first for all the cheering. He acted like an opera singer, strutting over and gesturing dramatically. His guitar was strapped to his back under his poncho, so he looked like a hunchback.

We killed ourselves, and Dar fell right over. I thought I'd pee my pants! And then the most amazing thing happened. Jesus threw off his poncho, walked straight to me, touched Dar and I on our shoulders, and asked us to shuffle apart so he could stand between us! Droplets of rain hit my face and arms, rain that'd slid down off his dripping ringlets. That's where I was for the whole campfire, sitting right next to him, staring at the mud splotches on his pant legs!!!

When it was over, just as everyone was getting up to go, he said "You've got an exceptional voice." That's how he said it, just like that: "You've got an exceptional voice." I was so stunned and like a dolt, all I could do was look at my feet and say "Oh."

"Do you take singing lessons?" he asked. "Or play an instrument?"

"Well, my dad's a rock musician and he used to be with the Blind Boas and I don't know if you've heard of them but he's taught me some music and the guitar and I did take piano lessons but I would never practice enough so this coming fall I'm taking a year off at least that's how Mom and Dad put it since they said they wouldn't have the energy to keep after me which is just fine because I'd rather sing and play guitar anyway and maybe I should be putting all my practice time into the guitar."

My eyes wandered up to his face. He was looking at me oddly, scratching his beard. He took off his guitar and turned to pack it. "Well, good luck with all that. A good voice is such a gift."

All the while Dar and Ali and Sheila were watching with big eyes and the occasional elbow poke.

"Well, gotta go I guess," I said to the back of his head.

"Take care," he replied over his shoulder.

"You toooooo!" I yelled, as my girlfriends and I ran across the hall to grab our coats and boots. By now they were giggling immaturely. "Shut up you guys," I shouted in a whisper. We scurried out into the rain, slapping through puddles back to the cabin.

That night we were the ones who hogged the

spotlight from the Cools, telling everyone what had just happened with Jesus and me. We agreed unanimously that he was the cutest guy on the planet and wasn't it too bad he was so old. (This we knew because Sidney and the Cools had swarmed him one night and bugged him until he confessed: He'd just turned twenty-three.)

"But he's only seven years older than the counselors, hey Sam," Sidney teased. Sam shook her head, but in her smile I could see she had the serious hots for him. It was a good thing that as an almost-minister he probably wasn't supposed to date girls like her. She wouldn't be his type anyway.

All night the rain tapped on the roof and all night I thought about how Jesus was ten years and three months older than me, which was almost exactly the difference in age between my grandparents – my mom's parents. It was a sign.

I dreamed about him all night, heard him say over and over, "You have an exceptional voice." By morning I was exhausted but happy.

In the drizzle of Friday we huddled in one muggy hall or another, making dream catchers and medicine bags, or eating bannock and bison burgers. Dar and Ali, and our two First Nations counselors, taught us a ceremonial dance, like they perform at powwows. It was fun, but everyone was really tired of being crowded into places that were too small for all of us.

Finally, finally, finally, there was one short, sunny break and Free Time was declared. Groups of girls were strolling here and there without raincoats, or sitting on their porches gabbing. Mandy and I had made a plan to meet at the Tuck Shop. I told her what had happened with Jesus. I didn't care if she told the whole world.

"Oh my gosh," she said, grabbing my wrist. "That is so incredibly fantastic!!! He is so incredibly cute. I can't believe it. Didn't I tell you you'd love the campfires? Didn't I?"

"Yeah, yeah, yeah," I said, trying to wipe the smile off my face.

"So, glad you came? Aren't you glad there's another week to go?"

"Okay, okay, I'm glad. So? It still wasn't right, how I was forced to come. As my best friend, you should've stuck up for me."

Mandy said nothing; her way of saying "I win."

We were about to step up to the Tuck Shop window when a piercing scream came through the trees, then shouts and hollers. The line of girls stopped talking, looked toward the commotion, and then, like we shared the same brain, everyone broke into a sprint and dashed down the road into the Bowl. A crowd had already gathered at Mandy's cabin.

We zipped around the puddle-lake and stood at the back of the group. Counselors were yelling at us to go to our cabins, but no one moved. Mandy pushed her way through with me holding on to the back of her T-shirt till we came out the other side where she whispered, "Oh, no. I just knew this was going to happen."

There was Snobbypants, sobbing. She was pressed up against the screen door as Bonnie skewered her with pointy tree branches, one at her ribcage, the other at her thigh. With each twist Snobbypants whimpered, obviously terrified.

Nearby on the porch were Mrs. Gormley, Tanya, and Poobah, who spoke gently. "It's okay Bonnie. Just be calm. No one wants to hurt you. We love you. You don't want to make Christine cry, do you?"

Tanya called softly, "Bonnie, it's Tuck Shop time. Want some ice cream?"

Bonnie didn't move.

"Mrs. Poobah! Mrs. Poobah!" someone shouted from the crowd. Poobah didn't flinch, her eyes locked on Bonnie. "Mrs. Poobah!"

The voice was right behind me now and I turned to see Lori pushing her way through. She had streaks of paint on her face, and her baseball cap said "Hot Chick." Mrs. Gormley tried to shush her, wave her away, but Lori ignored her.

"Mrs. Poobah," she said, breathless, "I help. Let me help," and without waiting for an answer she stepped right in behind Bonnie, her head barely as high as Bonnie's shoulder. Snobbypants winced, expecting to be stabbed, and the crowd gasped, but Lori reached around Bonnie's middle and held on, her head resting on Bonnie's back. In a few moments it was as if the two of them together were radiating a green-gold glow that got brighter and brighter. This time I was the one who gasped, and Mandy and I exchanged a look of stunned amazement. Bonnie dropped the sticks and Snobbypants ran into the arms of Mrs. Gormley, shaking and weeping. Poobah joined Lori in hugging Bonnie and the three of them disappeared into the cabin.

"Okay, everybody," shouted several counselors, "break it up. Break it up. Let's go!"

As the crowd dispersed, and Mandy and I made our way to the Mess Hall, it began raining again. Even so, I felt a big smile coming on. What Lori had done to calm Bonnie had been something wonderful – something of wonder. A strange excitement danced in my belly, and for a moment I had the urge to run back and see what was going on in Mandy's cabin. I wanted to know what else Lori was capable of.

"Wasn't that incredible?" I finally said.

"It sure was. I thought Christine was going to end up like a shish kabob, but that Lori knew just what to do. It was like magic."

"But it *was* some kind of magic." Mandy looked at me and raised her eyebrows. "You know, the glow thing…"

"Glow thing?"

"Yeah, the greenish halo all over their bodies."

"Really? You saw that?"

I paused, looked away from her. Was she kidding me? How could she have missed it?

"Never mind," I said with a shrug, "it must've been the way the sun shone through the leaves or something."

"Sure," she said. "Must've been."

Chapter 15

All I can say is thank God Mom stopped going to church. This was at the beginning of grade six. She had started the second in vitro process, said her hormones were all out of whack, and she was an emotional wreck. Sitting in a pew and thinking about life only made everything harder.

But Dad kept going. We had tried out three different churches in six years, but for two years we'd been at one that he called "liberal." He said it was the best fit. I heard him tell Mom he didn't agree with the pastors at the other churches. They reminded him too much of the small-town church he'd grown up in, which he called "totally weird." He liked where we were and he wanted us to stay connected, even if Mom refused to go.

So he made me go to Youth Group (what you join once you're in grade six and officially finished Sunday school). But I started to feel like I was faking it all the time, since we always started with a prayer, and I'd stopped praying because I already knew the truth: God doesn't always answer your most important prayers. God had helped other people, but wouldn't help us. By the end of grade six, after one failed in vitro and two lost pregnancies, that fact was absolutely, totally, one hundred percent clear. That was the first time I decided to be an atheist, but I didn't tell anybody.

But then, in mid-October at the beginning of grade seven, after I turned twelve, Mom got pregnant again. For the first three months we held our breath. We didn't allow ourselves to get excited, not even a bit. This time we didn't prepare at all for a baby. We pretended everything was normal. Mom started coming to church with us again. And even though I'd sworn off it, I couldn't help myself. I prayed. I worried if I didn't, I might jinx it and cause another miscarriage. Once I'd heard Gran James say a miscarriage was an act of God. Even though Dad had told me different, I heard myself asking God to please, please, please not commit another act of God. It was so confusing.

One day it occurred to me that Mom hardly ever talked about God. Maybe she was becoming an atheist too. So when Dad wasn't around I said, "Do you really believe in God?"

She looked at me for a long time. "That depends," she said.

"On whether or not you have a baby?" I replied.

"No. Depending on what you mean by God."

"Well, you know…God. The whole reason we have to go to church."

"I want to believe, Shannon, but let's just say I'm re-evaluating things. And if I ever figure out what I believe, I'll let you know."

By January 30, which was our deadline for when we'd allow ourselves to be happy and tell everyone, Mom was *still* pregnant! We ordered in from Yang's (our fave restaurant), and Dad said grace (which we don't normally do) and said thanks for the baby.

Then we planned who we'd tell and when. It was beyond exciting. We dared to say things like, "When the baby comes…" and "…little brother or sister…" and "There'll be a baby under the tree next Christmas." That night I had no problem saying thank you to God, who had come through in the end. We were buddies again.

My head was full of images of me and a baby and

our happy family of four, and of all the fun I'd have being a big sister. Everyone was so surprised and pleased for us. Mandy's eyes just about popped right out of her head.

"But your mom's so old!" she exclaimed. And compared to Mrs. Gormley she was, but I told her "There are lots of women who have babies in their forties." I was pleased to be able to educate her on the matter.

"Shannon James," she said, miffed, "I can't believe you didn't tell me sooner."

"I couldn't."

"But I wouldn't have told anyone."

"What about when you told Sue Morrison about Al Warner punching a teacher?"

"That's different."

I didn't argue. Deep in her heart of hearts she knew she would've blabbed.

Mom had already begun to swell up everywhere. No matter where we went people were so happy for us. They said how beautiful Mom looked, and it was true. In March she felt the baby wiggle for the first time. By April her belly skin was stretching and I felt the baby kick! Sometimes, watching TV, I'd lie with my cheek on her belly and feel it thumping away. It was so awesome! The due date was July 15, and it couldn't come fast enough.

Mom began having the most hilarious dreams. "It's

like going on an adventure every night," she said one morning. "There's so much going on at once, so much detail, and so many people moving in and out, I'm not sure I really get any rest at all."

It was kind of fun hearing the strange bits and pieces of her dreams. Sometimes Dad and I would be in them, but mostly it was strangers and places that were bizarre, like the coliseum in Athens. She had a job shooing away pigeons. Once it was a movie set where she was a stunt-woman, freaked out because she had to do dives and climb buildings while hugely pregnant.

One Saturday morning in June she came to the breakfast table looking terrible. "Feels like I've been awake all night," she said and adjusted her ruby house-coat around her enormous belly. "I dreamt I was flying, using my arms, and traveled to some other country. I floated into this mass of people." She stared at the table; didn't look at us like she usually did. "They were standing in a circle, several people deep. I passed through them to the middle. Someone was standing there and I floated around and around this figure and that's when the baby began to kick like a maniac. For real. Our little peanut's never been so active."

"Such a short dream kept you up all night?" Dad said and pushed a plate of oranges toward her.

"But I couldn't escape it. I kept trying to wake up, and then I'd be pulled back into it."

I buttered my toast. "That's all you did? Float around?"

"I don't remember much else. Oh, it was dark. There was just a little light on some faces. It wasn't really a nightmare, but it was unsettling."

"Thanks for the laugh," Dad said with his sideways smile.

"Anytime." The twinkle returned to her eyes. "So, missy, are you ready for the big move? 'Cause we could wait till next weekend if you want."

"M-o-o-o-o-m." I rolled my eyes. She knew very well I'd been packed for days. In just four weeks the baby would have my old, small room near theirs. Two carpenters had spent the last couple of weeks turning the attic into a beautiful, big bedroom, just for me.

Later that morning, Uncle Danny came over to help Dad move the heavy stuff. Mom and I unpacked and sorted. By Sunday night we were done. I stretched out on my bed and admired the colors I'd chosen: Vanilla and Wedgwood Blue. For years to come this'd be my private space. I imagined my little brother or sister as a toddler, coming up for a visit – or a sleepover. I'd read the little munchkin books and teach it everything

I already knew about everything. Thanks to me, it'd be the smartest kid in the world.

Chapter 16

On Friday evening the rain finally stopped. It was just after supper, and most campers didn't know it, but Bonnie was about to leave. Tanya had told just the girls in her cabin and Mandy had told me. So, when Bonnie's parents arrived, Mandy and I were nonchalantly doing a lot of nothing except peeking out through a bush near the parking lot where Bonnie's parents' car was parked.

"They're meeting up with Bonnie at the Gathering Hall," Mandy said, yanking at some wet leaves. "Tanya said we could go there and say good-bye."

"So, why aren't you there?"

"What's the point? Bonnie only talks to Tanya."

"Maybe Tanya's the only one who was nice to her."

"I was nice to her." She threw a handful of leaves to the ground. "But it's better that she's leaving."

Soon Bonnie and her parents were walking to their car. The parents looked like regular, normal people with tired faces. It made me feel extra sorry. Behind them were Poobah, Tanya, and Lori. We crouched a bit, which was stupid because we'd been trying to look like we were just hanging out, and now we looked like spies. When they opened the car doors Bonnie put her bag on the backseat and turned around to give Tanya a long hug. Then she hugged Poobah, and I watched really closely as she hugged Lori, hoping I wouldn't see the green-gold glow on them again. When there wasn't one I let out my breath. I had so far counted three bizarre events and I was starting to think I was losing it. Earlier that afternoon I had actually gone back to Mandy's cabin while the sun was out briefly, just to see how it might have shone down through the green poplar leaves and tricked my eyes. I was dismayed to see that the whole porch would have been shaded from the sun because of the way the roof came out over it. So, given that there was no glow thing between Bonnie and Lori now, I had to put it down to an over-active imagination.

Bonnie climbed into the backseat, Tanya and Lori

left, and Poobah leaned against the car. She crossed her arms over her chubby self and spoke quietly. The mom dabbed her eyes with a tissue and nodded. Her dad had his hands stuffed deep in his trouser pockets, and studied the ground. Soon they got in the car and drove away without returning Poobah's farewell wave.

"To tell the truth," said Mandy as we strolled toward the Gathering Hall, "if she'd stayed tonight she might've murdered us all in our sleep."

"I don't think so," I said, seeing the flaw in her statement. "Maybe she could've murdered one of you, but that person would've screamed and woken the rest up, so everyone else would've escaped."

Mandy looked at me like I had a point and I broke up. "For crying out loud," I whacked her arm, "nobody was going to murder anybody. That's the stupidest thing I've ever heard."

When we got to the hall for campfire, I just couldn't bring myself to sit next to Mandy. Something was different; something I couldn't describe. I just didn't want to be near her.

By some miracle I got to sit close to Jesus again. At first he didn't notice me because Dar and Ali were playing handheld drums and singing. Everyone whooped and hollered for them and then they got us up to do step dancing. I kept up with Jesus so that when we sat down again I was still near him. Just as he reached for his guitar, Poobah walked into the circle.

"Young ladies," she began, "in my seven years of running Camp Outlook, I've never had an incident such as the one today. And I've never had a camper leave early who wasn't sick to her stomach."

Tanya ran a knuckle under her eye. Next to her, Snobbypants picked at a manicured fingernail, and next to her, under the hat of a million pins, was a serious Mrs. Gormley, with her arm around Lori. But Lori didn't look sad like the rest of them. She was wearing another goofy ball cap, this time with little propeller sticking out of the top, and she kept reaching up to the top of her head to spin it. Our eyes met briefly, and that's when the fourth bizarre event occurred. I swear I heard her voice in my ears, saying "You're part of the circle." It wasn't like the day we made the praying hands, when I couldn't get the memory of her voice out of my head for a while. This time it was as though she was some kind of ventriloquist. Like, instead of sitting way over across from me, it was as if she was actually whispering it right into my ear. I glanced around to see if anyone else had heard it, but the rest of the girls were in that place you go to when you're about to be lectured to by an adult.

"Now ladies," Poobah continued, "I'm not going to lecture you, but I must repeat what was said on Day One: Camp Outlook is striving to be a truly *inclusive* camp."

There was a titter from the Cools who were probably whispering the usual joke: If our camp was so inclusive then why weren't boys allowed? Poobah glared at them.

"As I was saying, this means we celebrate *all* of God's children and we make *everyone* feel welcome. It means we open our hearts and minds to those with differences."

Poobah was speaking quietly, but I heard every word. My ears were prickling with the heat of shame, even though I'd had little to do with Bonnie. And then it happened again, "You're part of the circle. You're part of the circle." I shot a look at Lori, but she was already looking at me, right into my eyes. She smiled slightly and winked. *What the...?*

"Now, on behalf of the staff and myself, I want to say that we feel today's incident resulted from our inability to adequately prepare some of you, especially Bonnie's cabinmates, to live with someone with her particular differences. But some of you must also think hard about your role in Bonnie's unhappiness."

You could've heard a pin drop. Then Poobah made us close our eyes and say a prayer that I totally didn't hear. I didn't close my eyes. I stared at Lori again, but her head was down, eyes seemingly closed. Poobah's prayer went on and on. When it seemed Lori wasn't going to look at me again, I did close my eyes and suddenly, a movie began to play in my mind's eye: a boy is in a playground filled with kids, and they're playing on a climbing contraption with swings and slides. The boy tries to join in, but each time he tries, the kids move away from him. He looks so lonely, but he keeps grinning and waving and trying to catch up to them. Then the children pick up stones and begin to throw them at the boy, laughing, pointing, slapping one another on the back.

Suddenly I realized who the boy in my mind-movie was. It came so out of the blue; hit me smack in the chest, and the next thing I knew I was tucking my head down so no one would see I was bawling. But I let out a sob and my body began shaking. I couldn't help myself. Someone poked me in the shoulder and I looked up to find Jesus crouched next to me.

"C'mon. Let's go."

As Poobah ended her lecture-prayer with "Amen" he whisked me out the door, then leaned back in to yell, "Go ahead without me!"

On the front steps he gave me his cloth hanky. "It's clean," he said with a smile. I wiped my eyes, but no way was I going to use it to blow my nose. I sniffed a really good sniff (his hanky smelled lovely) and hoped to the high heavens my nose was clean. I just wanted to die. Die, *die, DIE.*

In the hall they started to sing "One Bottle of Pop" very, very loudly and very, very out of tune. I folded his hanky neatly, then held it out to him. I couldn't get up the nerve to look him in the face. He touched my fingers when he took it. "So, wanna tell me what's up?"

"Nothing," I replied, "I just feel bad for Bonnie."

"Did you know her?"

"Not really, just talked to her once. She was different, that's for sure."

"Autism'll do that to you," he said, then hooked his thumbs in his pockets. "What's your name?"

"Shannon James."

"Nice to meet you Shannon. I guess you know I'm Brad," and then he chuckled, "but I hear you girls call me Jesus."

"How'd you know?" I said. I could've kicked myself. My response was a dead giveaway that I was one of those girls.

"I have my ways," he said with this certain kind of smile that made my underarms go supremely itchy. My body turned toward the door without me even deciding that I should leave. I wanted to get away and stay standing next to him at the same time. You could say I was discombobulated, which is what my mom says she is a good deal of the time.

"Shannon." I turned back to him. "Are you sure you're okay?" And that's when I made the big mistake of looking right into his eyes, and he was looking at me with intense concern and I felt my heart explode and that's when I knew I could no longer call him Jesus, even as a little joke. That was the one thing I knew for sure, for sure.

I barely remember going back into the hall and joining the circle again. This time I sat in the back row and far away from where Jesu – *Brad* – had set down his guitar. Some people stared at me. Sam came over and sat next to me and put her arm around me, and I thought it was very nice of her to do that. I decided to sing, but only to help me erase three things: the sad movie from my mind, Lori's voice from my ears, and finally, Brad from my heart. When I crawled into my bunk that night, I'd had zero success erasing any of them.

I faced the wall while the Cools nattered on about all the cool things they'd do when they got home to their cool friends and cool lives. I was glad I didn't have to go home now; was actually glad to have another week at camp. Mandy and I would hang out all day Saturday, help with the cleanup for the incoming campers. The next campfire wouldn't be for forty-five hours. What would Brad do on his night off?

The next morning after breakfast the Bowl buzzed with activity, and the shouts of campers, counselors and parents picking up their daughters. Mandy and I sat on the yellow porch, enjoying the sun and watching the last group photos being taken. I'd already said good-bye to my cabinmates, signed everyone's autograph books, exchanged hugs and text addresses with Dar, Ali, and Sheila.

I hugged my knees, studied an ant hauling a huge leaf across the ground. My brain was filled with Brad, and I so wished Mandy could keep a secret. Then she elbowed me in the ribs and nodded towards the parking lot.

My jaw dropped. There was my dad striding across the Bowl, breathless and grinning. "Shannon! Shannon! Surprise!"

I grabbed him tight around the waist and he kissed the top of my head. "We've missed you, Shan."

I had a sickening feeling in my gut and my prediction was exactly right. He looked me in the eyes and said kindly, "I've come to take you home."

Chapter 17

I remember everything about our baby's arrival. Grade seven was finally over. The next three hot, hot weeks I hung with Mandy, often at the pool. Mom's due date came and went. And then, on July 19, when I arrived home for supper, Uncle Danny greeted me at the door with a huge smile and I went bananas!

"The baby?!?!?! Did the baby come?!?!?!"

"On its way," he said. "Your mom's water broke an hour ago."

"*Yessss!*" I squealed, pumping my fist. Uncle Danny laughed at me, but I didn't care. I zipped around like a maniac, grabbing my stuff and babbling. Under my bed

I'd hidden a plush bunny I'd bought with my allowance. I stuffed it into my backpack.

That night, in my cousin Susan's room, I couldn't sleep. I kept imagining what my parents were doing based, of course, on reality TV. Some of the baby shows were terrifying. I wondered if Mom was currently screaming her head off, or calmly breathing and counting and pushing. I wondered if Dad had to put his head between his knees again, like he'd done when I was born.

At breakfast the phone rang. This was it! But no, Dad just wanted to report that everything was going super-slow, that Mom was a real trooper, and he'd call again later. Now he had to call my grandma and grandpa in Vancouver to update them on Mom's progress. My grandpa was in a seniors' home and not doing too well, so we hoped the excitement of a baby would make him feel better.

Auntie Margot and I stayed by the phone all day. Meanwhile, Uncle Danny drove to Tisdale and picked up Gran James.

About nine that evening Dad called to say the baby wasn't going to come naturally, so Mom would be having a C-section. (Something gross and painful. I saw it on TV.) He told us to come to the hospital in an hour, so, for sure, July 20 would be our baby's birthday.

We waited for what seemed a double eternity, sitting around on the back deck because it was so stinking hot in the house. We watched the sprinkler go back and forth on the garden, not saying much. And then finally, just as it was getting really dark, my uncle, aunt, grandma, and I left my oldest cousin in charge, and we drove to the hospital. We waited in the "Families Only" room until just before midnight, when in walked Dad, his hair and clothes all mussed up and his face whiskery and pale. He gave me the biggest, tightest, longest hug ever. "Shan," he said, shaking, and a little choked up, "You've got a little brother." There were tears in his eyes, like he wanted to cry, but he needed to be manly.

"*Woohoo!!*" I hugged him again. "What's his name?"

"Don't know yet." He reached out to hug the rest of the family. And then he explained we wouldn't actually get to see our baby right then. He'd been taken away by the nurses because he had goop in his lungs that had to be sucked out. Nothing serious.

"Tomorrow," he said, "tomorrow morning you'll meet him. But come and see Mom. She's been missing you."

We followed him to the recovery room and there she was, flat on her back under blankets. Her face was a super-puffed-up-version of my mom, with pale skin, white lips, and incredibly greasy hair. Tubes and wires poked out everywhere. My stomach lurched. She turned her head and smiled, saying, "I'm so sorry you couldn't see him tonight. He's so beautiful. The most gorgeous little eyes." And then her own eyes let go tears of happiness. Each of us gave her a kiss and Gran James held her hand while we talked about the difficult experience. Then Dad got out his cell and called up my other grandma so Mom could give her the good news.

That night Dad slept on a cot in Mom's room, and I had another sleepover with my cousins. We got up early and went back to the hospital. Mom and Dad met us outside the Neonatal Intensive Care Unit, and did they look terrible or what? Mom was still in a gown and Dad, who'd barely slept, was pushing her in a wheelchair. Her hair was still greasy and flat – she hadn't bathed for three days! And her whole body was swollen up like a broiled sausage just before you pop the skin. She said it was from all the extra fluids she got through the IV.

They'd been up since six-thirty. Mom had tried to nurse the baby for the first time, but wasn't able to, so they gave him formula instead. And, they said they took a good look at our baby's little face and chose the name Gabriel. Gabe for short. I thought it was a gorgeous name. I remembered it from Sunday school.

"Gabriel was an angel," I said.

"That's it, Shan, the angel," Dad said. He cleared his throat and explained that we'd have to see Gabriel one at a time. I got to be first. Dad showed me the special way to wash my hands, and then I followed my parents into the ward.

It was a huge room full of nurses and incubators. In each one was a little bit of flesh and bones that sometimes hardly looked like a baby. Our Gabriel was one of the chubbier ones because he was six pounds twelve ounces. His arms lay out flat at his sides like a cross. His body was bundled in a light blanket. It was hard to appreciate his sweet face because a tiny tube came out of his nostril and another with two prongs was taped under his nose. Mom explained the prongs were for oxygen and the other was for feeding. When she said the formula went *through his nose* into his stomach, I gagged.

I placed the bunny-gift in the bassinette. A nurse got a chair for Dad and me, then put Gabriel in my arms, being careful with the tubes and wires that ran here and there. He slept through it all.

"So, Shan, can you believe it?"

I just smiled and smiled and couldn't speak. Mom had tears pouring down her face. All I knew was I just wanted to hold him forever, but I only had ten minutes.

Dad took a picture, and with the last flash I felt Gabe wriggle, so I looked down to find his startled, eyes staring straight up at me. They were ocean blue. He looked at me like I was from Mars, and even though people say that newborns can't really see, I'm sure he saw me. I held him closer and kissed his fat cheek gently.

"He is *sooooo* cute," I cooed. "I can't wait till he comes home."

My aunt, uncle and gran met Gabriel and returned to the waiting room with huge smiles. We agreed he was the most beautiful, most perfect baby ever.

That evening after supper, Dad picked me up at my cousins' and took me home. Now he'd be sleeping in his own bed, but Mom would be staying at the hospital to be closer to Gabriel, and also because of her C-section. (She showed me where the surgeon had actually stapled – STAPLED!!!!! – her belly closed with twenty-eight huge thick staples. Ouch!)

Dad called friends and relatives. The first were short chats, but the last one was to my Auntie Carol in Australia (his older sister). Up until then he'd sounded cheerful and excited about Gabriel, but with my auntie, after they'd talked for a while his voice cracked and she must've noticed because I heard him say, "No, everything's fine" and then he promised to call again soon.

When he saw my list of friends to call he went, "Whoa, you don't expect to phone them all tonight, do you?" We argued over how late I was allowed to make calls and I squeezed in ten before nine-thirty. In the end I started with Mandy, but I made her triple-promise she'd wait twenty-four hours before she told anyone else so she wouldn't "steal my thunder" as my mom says about the behavior of people like Mandy. It was a thrill to tell everyone what Gabe looked like and all that had happened.

At bedtime Dad came in to say goodnight. He sat at the end of my bed looking so tired. He still hadn't shaved or even taken a bath and he smelled bad.

"In the morning we'll hang out here for a while and then I have a few errands." His voice was flat. "We'll go see your mom and the baby in the afternoon."

When he left I lay in the dark and felt sad for us both. This wasn't the way I'd imagined the beginning of our new life. I'd pictured us, the four of us, arriving home together and getting busy with baby stuff, like giving baths and cuddling and feeding and comforting. There'd be excitement and laughter and lots of people dropping in to visit, and I'd be running around being the hostess since my mom wouldn't be able to. I'd have to take responsibility for lots and lots of stuff.

Instead the house was quiet, hollow. In my parents'

bedroom the empty bassinette was an eerie sight. My dad was looking more and more like his best friend had just died. I thought he was missing Mom and Gabe or he was just terribly exhausted. As I dozed off, little did I know that I'd just had my last day ever of being part of a normal family.

Usually, once I get to sleep I don't wake up till morning, but with all that had happened I wasn't in my regular comatose state. I heard the stairs creak and moments later the microwave beeped. I checked the clock: 3:14 in the morning. Nudging my bedroom door open, I tiptoed to the top of the stairs, avoiding all the squeaky spots. I froze and listened hard. Dad was probably making hot milk. Then I heard something I'd never heard before, a kind of gut-wrenching moan, the sound a man would make if he really wanted to howl but didn't want anyone to hear him. Then there was another. And another. My heart stopped and I had to tell myself to breathe or I might keel over. I don't even remember going down the stairs, just that suddenly I was in the kitchen. Dad was sitting with his head in his hands, his long hair loose over his shoulders, shaking and crying. Without looking up he said, "You're supposed to be in bed. Asleep." I stood and waited and waited until he looked at me. I had no words in my pea-brain at all.

"Sit down." I did and watched him wipe his face with a tea towel. He sipped his mug of milk, looking at the floor. It took a long time before he said, "I was going to tell you in the morning."

"Tell me what?"

"About Gabriel."

"What about him?"

"Well…well, your little brother…" His voice trailed off and he wept a little. "Your little brother…isn't…isn't a…a…normal baby."

"Is he sick?"

"No, no, not exactly. But he's…he's got something…. It's called Down syndrome."

And that's when I knew for certain I couldn't possibly believe in God anymore.

Chapter 18

Here's the thing: Dad coming to camp to take me home early was my own stupid fault. I'd spoken to my parents three times on Mrs. Gormley's cell, which she had nagged me to do because my parents had nagged her to make me.

I mostly asked them about Gabriel, who had been twelve days old when I left for camp. I really did want to know how he was, this being his third week in Neonatal. They were visiting him four times a day. He was gaining weight and nursing better. They finally got to give him a bath instead of a nurse doing it. And some nights my mom was able to sleep at home.

Once I did ask how Mom was feeling, but otherwise I behaved like a jerk on the phone. I wanted them to know I wouldn't easily forgive them for sending me away. So, when they asked me about camp I made it sound horrible. They'd say "Are you making new friends?" and I'd say "Don't like anybody." Or they'd say "What have you been doing?" and I'd say "Nothing fun; they make us do stupid crafts, and it's raining so much you can't even swim. It really sucks." And then they'd lecture me about using the word *sucks* and I'd say "Whatever," and they'd sigh and I'd say "Gotta go."

Still, I never thought in a million years that they'd change their minds about me staying at camp for the full two weeks. The rule around our house was if you signed up for something, then you weren't allowed to quit just willy-nilly.

But, there was Dad, large as life, intending to take me home.

Mandy said, "Aaaw Mr. James, that's too bad. She's having such a good time," and Dad looked at me as if to say "Really?" My brain was about to explode. I couldn't admit I was happy. The idea of my parents knowing they'd been right all along was just too hideous to contemplate.

"I'll go pack," I told him. I went to my cabin and

totally freaked out. I pounded my mattress till the dust flew. I said several swears that I will not repeat. Yes, I wanted to see Gabe again. Yes, I wanted to be treated like an adult and be with my folks during this terrible crisis. But I'd have to leave Brad. How could one major heart explosion totally take control of you like that?

I threw everything into my suitcase. I kicked the foot of the bunk bed, nearly breaking my toe. I zipped my bag and stuffed my reading book into the side pocket. And that's what gave me my brilliant idea!

I dashed back to Mandy's cabin. Dad was on the front step talking intensely to Mrs. Gormley. "Where's your bag?"

"It's packed," I said, hoping Mrs. Gormley would go, but she wouldn't, so I said, "I need help. I've got a lot of crafts."

Mrs. Gormley stood up and gave me a good-bye hug, holding tight to her hat of a million pins. I dragged Dad to my cabin, and once we were inside I said, "While I was packing I was thinking hard about leaving, and... well...Dad...you shouldn't have forced me to come, but now that I'm here it would be better if I stayed."

"Oh? I thought you hated it," he said, suspiciously. "I drove all the way here because you sounded absolutely miserable."

"I'm sorry, Dad, but I'm just thinking about Dianne Wimsworth's book and how she said it's not so good for kids to be forced to move around too much. We're supposed to have a stable environment. It's better for us. Emotionally speaking."

His eyebrows practically hit his hairline. "She was probably talking about kids whose parents are divorced."

"But she said kids who suddenly do strange things – and I did do some strange things recently – sometimes do them because there's been a big change and so they need to have everything just the same for a while so that they aren't so stressed out so I think I should stay here instead of experiencing another big change by going home."

He looked at me like he thought I was on drugs. "That makes no sense at all, my girl, but obviously something's happened to make you want to stay, so, okay. Stay. Your mom will be disappointed. She was looking forward to having you home again."

On the outside I tried to look like I was giving this a second thought, but on the inside I went, "Yesssss!" As I collected up my crafts from my little shelf and loaded them into Dad's arms I said, "Please tell Mom I understand now. It's better for her to focus on Gabriel, especially with his extra problems." And then it only seemed right to say, "I'm sorry for making you drive all the way here. I'm sorry for getting into such big trouble at the mall, for being such a pain generally."

Dad shrugged, but seemed to be okay with my apology. Before he went home we drove into Outlook for lunch and I had my eyes peeled for you-know-who. In the restaurant Dad said Mom was with Gabe as much as possible and the slit in her belly was feeling better. They were beginning to get used to the idea of having a child with Downs. He said when I got home we'd get some counseling as a family to help us adapt to our new lives.

"But I don't want a *new life*." I stabbed at my fries. "I want my *old* life, with the addition of a baby brother. A *normal* baby brother."

"Believe me, I understand," he replied, and then he changed the subject.

That night Mandy and I shared a cabin, just the two of us. (Sam and Tanya and some other counselors stayed overnight, too, since they'd be working the next week. They were next door and super-rowdy. Around midnight we heard Poobah giving them one of her non-lectures.) Mandy and I blabbed till two in the morning, with Mandy doing most of the talking. She gossiped about everyone who'd been in her cabin. I had lots of secrets I could've talked about, like Gabe, or Brad, or what I'd recently done at the mall, but there were things I no longer wanted her to know about me. We'd been best friends for five years so I'd already forgiven a lot of little things she had done that bugged me. But now there was something bigger that bugged me, something I didn't quite understand. It didn't make me feel good thinking about it, so instead I counted the number of hours until campfire (nineteen), and I drifted off to sleep.

In the morning we helped her mom peel a million potatoes. Ten hours to campfire. We helped with cabin cleanup. Eight point five hours to campfire. We had a sandwich lunch with the counselors and employees, and Poobah gave the registration details. Then Mandy and I had to leave so they could discuss private things. Seven more hours.

At two o'clock we were the first to register, since we'd be official helpers for the afternoon. This time I'd be in the green cabin with Tanya as my counselor. Mandy got red and a new counselor named Rachel.

For a few hours girls arrived loaded down with backpacks and suitcases and sleeping bags. Mandy and I stood in the parking lot and directed everyone to the Gathering Hall.

"Hey, there's Cindy from last year," Mandy said, waving at her. "Cindy! Cindy! Hi!"

They ran to each other and did a totally juvenile

hopping dance, but whatever. She greeted others like that too. If you come here for five years in a row you get to know people. She even knew this one girl who wore a leg brace and had a deformed arm, but intellectually she was fine. After the girl had gone, Mandy told me she'd been born that way and weren't we lucky not to be her. For a brief moment our eyes met and we knew something had changed; she should not have said that.

By four o'clock we were at our cabins for introductions and camp rules. Just a week earlier it had been Sam talking to us, and I'd been planning to run away. Now there was nowhere else I wanted to be, and it was Tanya yelling to get our attention.

"Green cabin! Green cabin! Yoohoo! Get over here please!"

This camp wasn't sold out like the first week, so there weren't as many girls in our group. We could all fit on the porch, and went around the circle giving our names: Sophia, Regan, Jocelyn, Piper, Debbie, Patti, and me. Tanya checked us off from a list on her clipboard and just as she said, "Mmm, we're still missing Ella," up walked a tall, gray-haired lady. Someone was hiding behind her.

"Sorry to interrupt," she said to Tanya, "and we're so sorry to be late."

"That's fine," Tanya replied. "You must be Mrs. Stevens."

"Yes, and this is my daughter Ella." She reached behind her back and pulled the girl out. It was immediately obvious she had Downs. She looked more like Gabriel's sister than I did. It felt weird.

The woman stroked her daughter's thick, long hair. "Ella, say hello."

"'Lo," she said.

"Hello," we all replied.

"I'm at cump. Cump Howtlook."

"Yes you are," Tanya said. "Would you like to hold my hand?" Ella did so, happily, and Tanya went, "We're going to have some fun together, Ella."

The faces of my cabinmates told a different story. It was probably on my face, too. *Bonnie, Bonnie, Bonnie.*

Tanya led her to the steps and invited her mom to stay to help Ella settle in. We shuffled over and gave them lots of room to sit down.

As she'd done with Bonnie, Tanya took Ella under her wing. Over supper Ella stayed close to Tanya. Meanwhile, the rest of us got to know each other. Only one girl had been to Camp Outlook before, but three years earlier, so she was way out of date. She didn't know anything about Brad and how fantastic he was at campfire. I was happy to fill them in. I did not mention his nickname.

That night Brad rocked, and all the new girls were crazy about him. However, Sam ruined the evening by constantly ogling him. She no longer cared if she got fired because she was dressed totally sleazy. Unfortunately, Brad's super-willpower was disintegrating. He flubbed his words every time he looked her way.

As if that wasn't enough, I began having head problems: Bizarre Event Number Five. I started hearing voices during the sing-along, after we'd sung several songs and then had started into "Four Strong Winds." These were voices that weren't singing with everyone else around the fire. They weren't even singing words, just beautiful sounds. For a while I didn't realize this was going on. I just felt overwhelmingly happy. I thought the music was being made by people in the group, the way you sometimes can hear a person or two making up a harmony on the spot in a crowd of singers, maybe at a church or a concert or something. I could always pick out that sound because of what my dad had taught me about harmonies, and it would make me feel something inside that always made me smile for the beauty of it. But after a minute or so I realized the voices weren't singing the same song, and some voices were high, like little kids, others low like adults. And every once in a while I'd hear someone speak, and they'd say, "It belongs to all of us." Sometimes it was clear, sometimes not. Sometimes a child's voice, sometimes a man or woman. I felt all discombobulated, not knowing what to make of it, so I put my head down on my knees for a few minutes, and even when the campers started a new song, the singing voices continued and "It belongs to all of us" was getting louder and louder in my head till I couldn't stand it anymore. I looked up and I accidentally made eye contact with Ella. What happened next freaked me out completely. Just as I heard a child's voice in my head go, "It belongs to all of us," Ella's lips moved, mouthing exactly the same words at exactly the same time. *Exactly* the same. I swear.

And when she looked away, the voices vanished.

Chapter 19

When we started grade seven, Mandy and I were finally allowed to go to the mall by ourselves. We mostly went on Saturdays. We'd catch a movie or just sit in the Food Court being adult-like.

So, last spring, Mandy started inviting Sue Morrison along. Sue had a crush on Mandy's grade nine brother, but it didn't seem to bother Mandy that she was really being used by Sue. Mandy just liked being around her because she was one of the Cools, which made Mandy feel cooler herself. She practically drooled over Sue's every word. It was sickening.

The thing about Sue was she'd sit in the Food Court

and make fun of people, especially the group of adults who showed up every Saturday from a care home. (You sometimes hear them called *special* or *retarded,* but I've since learned some people don't like those words.) As we sat eating our fries, Sue'd say things like "Sure glad I'm not one of them," or make jokes about the way they looked and dressed, or mimicked the way they talked. Mandy and I giggled uncontrollably. When she said she didn't know how the caregivers could stand working with them, I'm ashamed to admit I agreed. I thought it wasn't something I'd ever want to do.

Sue seemed pretty funny until the one Saturday we were lined up for ice cream, standing in front of some of those people. Sue was horsing around, being exceedingly juvenile, and she shoved me into one of the guys so hard he had to grab me to break my fall. For the rest of the afternoon Sue accused me of having retard-cooties. I didn't laugh, but Mandy did.

Honestly, his rough hands on my skin had creeped me out. He was really strong and held me tight for too long. I had noticed him many times before because he always looked like he was having a good time. His small eyes crinkled up with glee, his thick tongue stuck out a bit. He had Down syndrome.

When I held Gabriel for the second time ever, I

thought about that man. I could now see in my brother what I hadn't noticed the day before: slanted eyes, small nose, tongue sticking out. But in so many other ways he appeared so normal.

Mom was in her wheelchair and she put her arm around me as I cradled him, his tubes and wires running down my lap.

"He won't look like us," I blurted, not thinking how it'd make her feel. She just nodded. "He'll look like himself. But he might look like us. He does actually look a lot like you when you were a baby. Exact same hair color, for one thing." But I kept seeing the man in the mall, his oddly shaped, chubby body, at times looking kind of dopey. The thought of me going places with someone like him, out where your friends could see you, made me suddenly sick to my stomach. For the billionth time in twelve hours I thought, *This cannot be happening. This cannot be happening.*

"You can hardly tell he's got Downs," I said hopefully. "Maybe we don't have to tell anybody. For now."

"Oh, Shannon, soon enough it'll be obvious."

Gabe squawked extremely loudly for such a tiny being. Mom lifted him from my arms. "I'll try nursing him again."

But he looked so helpless, unsure of what to do with

his mouth. When he wouldn't latch on, Mom sighed and said, "He's not strong enough, but yesterday I talked to another mom who assured me most of these babies can do it. You have to persist."

"Another mom?"

"Yeah, a nurse connected me with someone who has a child like Gabe. She had to try a hundred different tricks, but she did it. *They* did it."

Just as Gabriel seemed to be getting a few good slurps of milk, his nurse said time was up, that his whole feeding schedule would be thrown off if she didn't feed him through his nose immediately. My mom was really ticked off.

When we met up with Dad in the waiting room, she was fuming and totally stressed and completely discombobulated when she tried to explain what had just happened, so I had to explain it. (And get this: because Gabe wasn't drinking properly, Mom had to pump the excess milk out of herself with a machine, just like you'd milk a cow!!! This added to her general crabbiness, especially when she couldn't get much out.)

Back in her room (which was all decorated with flowers from friends who had no idea about Gabe's condition) Dad helped her take off her housecoat and get into bed. It was extremely painful to do because of the incision and all the staples. They argued about whether or not they should just take Gabe home right then and there, so Mom could nurse him in peace, until there was a knock, and in barged the neonatal doctor.

"Oh good," he said, "you're here." He pulled over a chair and plunked himself down.

"The tests we did this morning," he said flipping through his file, "are back." With his pen he pointed at an X-ray-thing (which didn't look like anything to me). "There's a hole in Baby's heart, right here. You see? So this will require an operation in a few months. We send all our pediatric heart patients to Edmonton."

Dad reached for Mom's hand. I had just seen Gabe naked for the first time. He was so puny. How would they ever get into his tiny chest to operate? Break his little ribs? Use a saw? I gagged.

"I'm sorry," the doctor went on. "The good news is that it's all completely routine now. Nothing to worry about."

Really?

He left, and Mom broke down. Dad told me to go watch TV in the family lounge. So I went and stared at the screen, but my head was full of so many other things. Like Gabe's face, how it was so beautiful, how happy it made me. But the next moment it hit me that now there was no possibility I'd ever be an auntie – Gabe would never have kids – and I felt sad and mad at the same time. Then I felt selfish about all that, thinking how he would grow up needing all the things any little brother would need, and how he really needed a sister to love him. Then I worried about his heart. Then I worried for our family because we weren't normal anymore, and we'd never be normal again.

Okay. So maybe I was mostly worried for me. I think I should be allowed to be worried about me.

Here's the thing: now I'd be The Girl With The Retarded Brother. That's how people at school would think of me. The one who has a retard for a brother. And the more I thought about it the angrier I got. I wanted answers. I wanted to know why God hated us so much. Why would God make us so happy by letting my mom get pregnant only to give us a baby like Gabe? The whole thing sucked, totally and completely. *IT SUCKED!!!*

Then I remembered that, as of last night, I'd become an atheist again, so all of my aforementioned stupid questions could just be flushed down the toilet, along with all my long ago prayers that some people thought were so important.

Soon Dad and I would be going over to my uncle's to tell him and Gran James about Gabe having Downs and now, the heart operation. I worried about Gran and how she'd take the news. She was an old lady who cried a lot. She'd cry over *Coronation Street* or when I sang a solo at church. Once, when I was seven, she'd taken me to a store in her town where they have one of those horse rides for kids. A strange looking girl was putting in her quarter. Gran's eyes got teary and she said, "Poor thing." She told me the girl was a Mongoloid, and then she said, "Actually, you aren't supposed to use that word anymore. You're supposed to say she has Down syndrome."

The mall-guy had been a baby once, too. Maybe he'd looked a lot like Gabe then. It'd never occurred to me that all the people with Down syndrome had at one time been tiny babies. It seemed you never saw too many babies around who had it. It was as if there were only adult versions of them on the planet. I wondered if he'd had trouble drinking his milk when he was a baby, and if he'd had a heart problem. When he and his friends came to the mall there were always a couple of regular people with them. So who had looked after the mall-guy when he was born? Did he have parents the way Gabe and I did? Or did he always live separate from regular people.

Before I could have any more big thoughts, Dad showed up to say Mom was trying to rest. It was time to go home. In the car I asked him if they were worried about the operation.

"Everything's going to be fine," he said. "Soon Gabe'll come home. Then we'll worry about his heart." He was quiet for a long time. Soon I noticed we were driving in the wrong direction.

"I thought we were going to Uncle Danny's."

"Oh, I thought you could start supper while I go," he said, faking cheerfulness, "maybe that bean casserole Mom taught you to make. You do it so well."

"Whatever," I replied.

"Don't be like that, Shan. This news'll be hard on them. You don't need to be there. Sorry."

I totally got it. This meeting would be too mature for my childish ears. I gave him the silent treatment until I got out of the car. You bet I slammed the door good and hard. I let myself into the house without waving and went straight to the phone to see if anyone had called. Sure enough it was blinking. I listened. There were tons of messages from people congratulating us on our *perfect* new baby. Dad hadn't mentioned the Downs to anyone. Said he wanted everyone to be happy for us, that Gabriel deserved to be welcomed to the planet as a person, not as a diagnosis.

Mandy'd left a message wanting to know when

Gabriel would be home. Maybe Mom was wrong. Maybe we wouldn't have to tell anyone ever that Gabe had Downs. He really did look normal. So far none of the family who'd met him had a sniff there was anything wrong with his brain or his heart or his face. How long could a person pretend? How long could you make others believe it, too?

I just wanted to give everyone more time to be excited for us like they were for every other family who has a baby. I wanted more time to pretend we were happy and normal. I wanted time for the sick feeling in my stomach and the numb feeling in my head to go away. My brain was working overtime, trying to figure out what to do; in fact my brain was so busy it didn't even notice me opening a can of beans, cranking, cranking, cranking the can opener handle around and around and around long after it was open. And my brain couldn't stop my hand from picking up the can and tipping it over in the middle of the kitchen counter to shake out a big mound of gooey brown beans.

The next thing I knew my feet were carrying me down Louise Avenue toward the mall, completely unable to stop myself, and about to do the worst thing I'd ever done.

Chapter 20

After Sunday night campfire, we were getting ready for bed in the cabin and I noticed several girls watching Ella. They were curious. So was I. Tanya helped her zip her sleeping bag and I tried not to gawk, but I was thinking about Gabe, what he'd be like at her age. I did the math. By then I'd be almost twenty-four. I might be married. Might even have a baby myself. Weird.

Ella's bunk was right across from mine. She turned on her side and stared at me. I stared back, remembering Bizarre Event Number Five. Her eyebrows and round eyes made her look permanently surprised. Her mouth hung open a bit showing her teeth, which were small and pointy. I rolled on my back, feeling a little sick. I was sorry to feel that way.

"Bafroom?" she said. Tanya was busy fixing a bunk spring.

"I can take her." It was Patti, the girl with pink streaks in her hair. "I help someone like Ella at my school all the time."

"Wonderful," said Tanya, handing Patti a big flashlight. No sooner did they leave than they were back again.

"Too duk," said Ella and plopped down on her bunk, genuinely terrified. Patti stood in the doorway going, "It's okay, Ella, I'll make sure you're safe. C'mon. Let's go." But she wouldn't move. The rest of us looked at one another, a couple rolling their eyes as if to say "Oh great, a whole week of this."

"But you have to," said Tanya. "Do you want to wet your bed?"

Ella shook her head, stood up, put one hand over her eyes and let Patti take her outside again, holding Ella's other hand.

While they were gone and everyone was talking, Tanya tidied Ella's bunk and put a few of her small belongings on her little shelf, including a picture she had brought of her mom and dad, and two teenagers who were older than Ella. Tanya moved around like a busy bee, looking very in charge of everything. She even swept the floor, although we'd only been in the cabin for a few hours. She was skinny and I'd noticed during the week how she liked to wear long shorts with plenty of pockets, and always wore at least two tight sleeveless shirts in layers with her bra straps showing, then several chain necklaces and a few bracelets. Now she was on her bunk, removing the jewelery and placing everything into a plastic box with dividers, all neat and organized. When she was ready for bed, she took a clipboard off a nail on the wall and began checking things off on a list. Just when I began to wonder what was taking Patti and Ella so long, we heard them talking out front and Patti came in, still holding Ella's hand.

"Good grief," Patti laughed, "Ella had to cover her eyes all the way to the outhouse and back, even though she kept tripping."

"I don't get it," said Regan, "if it's dark and she can't see anything anyway, why is she covering her eyes? That makes no sense."

"Actually, it's quite clever," said Tanya. "She's solving a problem. The dark makes her nervous, so she blocks it out. Problem solved."

Once everybody was tucked in Tanya made us play

a game. Each girl named three things that'd happened to her, but one of those things had to be a lie. Then everyone else had to ask her questions to figure out which event was untrue. It was a lot of fun and you got to know something about each person, like that Sophia once went to England and got to meet the queen, and Debbie once escaped from a house fire that almost killed her little sister, but that was ten years ago. Still, it was shocking. And Regan, she had recently won a prize for having the best science project in the province. No one tried to be supercool. Everyone seemed normal and nice.

It entered my head that one of my true events could be that I'd just become a big sister. But then I got scared about what kinds of questions they might ask if they knew, so instead, I chose two other true events: A long time ago, I got to hang out backstage with Wide Mouth Mason, which is a band most of my friends haven't heard of, even though they once opened for the Rolling Stones. And I won a thousand dollars when I was nine because my Grandpa James (before he died) bought me a two-dollar lottery ticket for my birthday. For my lie I said I once got to sing backup on a CD by the Hawks, which is a band my dad sometimes plays with, if they need a fill-in guitar player. I ended up winning because only Patti correctly guessed which was the lie.

During the game my eyes were glued on Ella. She seemed to follow what was happening, often laughing when we did. When she smiled she was actually very pretty. When she didn't, her face drooped a little and it was hard to read her, like she was on another planet. She was the last to play the game. At first she looked puzzled. I'm sure everyone thought she wouldn't be able to do it.

"Ella, tell us about something you did once," Tanya said softly.

Ella tipped her head, unsure what to say. We held our breath.

"Did you ever go on a holiday?"

"Cump Howtlook," she replied. Some of us smiled.

"Okay, but did you ever go on a trip with your family?"

"Mekico. We swum in the o-sea-en."

It seemed we all exhaled at once, and Patti, who was on the bunk over Ella, leaned over and said, "Hey Ella, I've been to Mexico too! We got to swim with dolphins," and Ella looked up at her with a huge smile and said, "Dolpins! Me too!" and the rest of us laughed, so then Ella laughed when she saw us laughing, which made us all laugh even more.

"So Ella," said Tanya, "now you get to tell us a lie."

"Lie?" she said. "Lies are bad. Don't evah lie." We stifled our giggles.

"Okay then," said Tanya, "can you pretend? What do you like to pretend?"

Ella took a moment, stroking her sleeping bag thoughtfully. "I like to fly."

Debbie shouted, "That's the lie – I win!" and Ella looked hurt. Seeing this, Tanya said, "You like to pretend to fly?" and Ella replied firmly, "No. I. Like. To. Fly." That's what she said. And everyone else heard it, too.

There was a rap on the door and Poobah's voice saying, "It's past eleven o'clock girls. Lights-out!" We burst into titters again and Tanya shouted, "Oops! Yep, sorry!" We wiggled deeper into our sleeping bags and adjusted our pillows. I glanced over at Ella and caught her staring at me again. Our eyes locked intensely. There was something major going on in her brain and I was relieved when Tanya turned out the lights.

We talked quietly, and it wasn't long before someone started to snore. Loudly. Another giggle-fit broke out. Tanya switched on the flashlight, shone it bunk to bunk, landing finally on Ella. She was dead asleep with her mouth open, snuffling.

"Is she okay?" whispered Regan and Tanya said, "Yeah, she just has respiratory problems. Her mom said she'd snore."

The flashlight clicked and in the dark, the talking

petered out. I listened to Ella's mouth-breathing and snuffling. Was she dreaming? What would a person like her
dream about? What would Gabe dream about? He could
be dreaming right then, in his bassinette in the hospital.
When he was Ella's age, would he go to the bathroom by
himself? Would he play games with other kids? Would he
understand when you asked him a question?

Deep down I knew if Gabe were a normal baby I'd
be blabbing about him constantly. A pang of guilt shot
through my chest and I remembered something Mom
had said to Dad: "Gabe's beautiful, and holding him
makes me so happy," she paused, then her voice went
high and sad, "but when I picture him as a teenager, or
an adult, out in the real world, that's when I fall apart."

I'd seen the looks between the girls in my cabin, the
signals saying it was too bad Ella was here. We were awkward, unsure how to be with her or what to say. How
often would people be like that with my little brother?
Suddenly I understood what my mom meant about the
real world.

This cabin was the real world.

I rolled over to face the wall and dried my face on
the pillow.

Chapter 21

When Dad got home from telling Gran and my uncle about Gabriel's problems he was *not* pleased to find beans all over the kitchen counter. He was even more ticked to discover I'd taken off. He was supposed to go back to the hospital after supper, but instead he had to hang around wondering if he should call the police. In the end it wasn't necessary because they called him.

When you're a kid, all kinds of people will tell you you've got choices in your life. They'll say you have opportunities to do lots of good things and lots of bad things. It's up to you to make the choice of what to do. Your parents will tell you that. Your teachers at school and church will tell you that. They'll all try to drill it deep into your brain. You have a choice. *You have a choice. YOU HAVE A CHOICE!*

But I beg to differ.

Sometimes you do *not* have a choice.

Sometimes you find yourself wandering around a big shopping mall, having just spilled a whole can of beans, where you're not supposed to, for no good reason. And you have these kinds of thoughts, the kinds of thoughts in which you believe you could actually just move into the mall and never go home again. You could find a corner not too many people know about, maybe back behind one of those doors that says STAFF ONLY and you could set up a little bed and a little place to store your clothes, which you would buy at the mall with the money you would (unfortunately) have to steal in order to survive. The Food Court would make eating very convenient. All the buses in the world stop there, so you'd have no problem going to school or visiting your friends. You could be having these kinds of thoughts as you're wondering around the mall and not be concentrating too well on things like right and wrong, and there you are in a music store staring at a CD by your current fave singer, and it seems like you have no choice but to slip the CD under your shirt because you're living in the mall, and you'll definitely need to listen to music in order to survive. And just as you're on your way back to your little corner hidden behind the STAFF ONLY doors, you are shocked and surprised to hear a great loud beeping in your ears, and suddenly someone grabs you from behind and hauls you back to the store, and you don't even feel all that embarrassed because it hasn't occurred to you that you've done anything wrong. You would've had to have had a choice for that to happen. A *choice*.

What I'd done didn't begin to sink in until I was sitting in the back office. Leo, the owner-manager (according to his nametag), was asking me a bunch of questions and writing down my answers when he said, "I need to fill this out before the police show up."

The word *police* snapped me back to reality. A slight tremble began in my knees and spread out until my whole body was shaking. I could barely answer the questions. By the time they arrived (Can you believe they sent *two* cops for one puny kid?) I was bawling my eyes out. Their names were Wentz and Miller, but I never knew which was which. One said, "Did you leave with the CD on purpose, or were you planning to pay for it and just forgot?"

"I didn't steal it," I blubbered. "I don't know why I forgot to pay for it."

"Do you have any money with you?"

I shut up.

"Miss James, do you have any cash on your person?" He was looking at me in a kind way, but he expected an answer. I shook my head, certain I would soon throw up.

"Could I please call my dad?" I pleaded. "I just want my dad."

Twenty minutes later they were sitting in our living room having serious words with Dad, who was pale and speaking slowly.

"Are you sure?" he said.

"She put it under her shirt," the one cop said. Then the other officer said the most beautiful words I've ever heard.

"On first offences we don't want kids going to court."

"Well, I certainly agree with that," Dad replied, refusing to look at me. "I believe, officers, that my daughter just made a serious error in judgment. She's a good kid. Really, she is."

Up till then I'd been watching the three men talking about me, but when my dad said I was a good kid I hung my head low, low, low. When the cops came over to say good-bye, it took all my will to stand up and look them in the eyes.

"This is your warning, Miss James," one said sternly.

"It won't go well for you if you're ever caught stealing again."

I nodded.

"What do you say to these gentlemen, Shan?"

"Thank you," I croaked.

The kinder cop smiled slightly and touched my shoulder. "We don't ever want to see you again."

The feeling was mutual, of course. Dad saw them to the door while I remained glued to my chair. When he came back I could tell he was trying really hard not to kill me. For one thing he stood as far away from me as possible. He crossed his arms and paced a bit, then froze. For a long time he just stared at me.

"So Shan," he finally said, calmly, just like Dianne Wimsworth says a parent should do during times of crisis. "You gonna tell me what this is all about?"

I looked for the words. He looked at his watch. Then he disappeared into the kitchen and something crashed onto the floor. I walked slowly to the doorway, peeked around it. He was forcefully scraping beans off the counter and plopping them into the sink. Sure enough, in the middle of the floor was an upturned chair. Doing that was so totally not my dad.

"I'm sorry," I whispered. "I'm sorry for everything, but I think I was having a Crisis Day like Dianne..."

"Crisis Day?" He dropped the spatula and glared. "Just what the hell were you thinking Shan? Just what the hell were you thinking? How could you do this when you know what your mother and I are going through? What is wrong with you? Hey? HEY? Have you lost your mind?!!!"

This is when it became clear that Dad should've actually read Dianne Wimsworth's book because he was now way off course regarding the treatment of kids during times of crises. You are not supposed to "belittle" your child, although I could certainly see why he'd want to belittle me. He went on and on.

"Just what am I supposed to do now, hmm? It seems I can't trust you on your own anymore, and I can't drag you along for every hospital visit. I was supposed to be there half an hour ago. You might recall we have a sick baby who needs heart surgery, for crying out loud. Remember that? REMEMBER THAT? Your mom is in such shock about everything that she's taking pills to sleep at night. She's a mess in every way. How can I tell her what you've done? And on top of that, I come home, after a very, very emotional time with your grandma and uncle and everybody over there – Do you have any idea how hard it was to break the news about Gabriel? – after all that, I come home to find these bloody beans all over the place and you out stealing stuff. ARE YOU INSANE?"

Of course, by this time I was blubbering away and thinking I probably *was* insane, if insane meant that you do things because you don't have a choice. If something takes you over and makes you do something, then maybe you *are* insane. This information I kept to myself, since things were bad enough without Dad putting me away. Instead, I said, "I'm sorry, I'm sorry. I'm sorry. You can leave me on my own. I promise I'll be good."

He just shook his head. "Go on, get your things. You'll come tonight and tomorrow I'll figure out what we'll do with you when I'm at the hospital. And not a word of this to your mother. Not a word. So stop your crying. I don't want her to suspect a thing. Understand?"

I nodded and grabbed my reading book.

At the hospital I gave my mom a huge long hug and tried to look happy and normal. Dad told Mom a white lie, which was that we were late because of telling Gran and his brother about Gabe.

"How'd they take the news?" She pressed the button on her bed that helped her sit up.

"They were pretty shocked, of course. He looks so... so...regular. They're going to call you later, but Mom said..." He paused to think manly thoughts to keep from crying. "She said to tell you that Gabe is a gift like any child, and God couldn't have chosen two better parents for him, and that...that...she has no doubt you'll be a fantastic mother."

Mom reached for the tissue box and we passed it around. I blew my nose hard. How could Gran James say such stupid things? How could she believe in a God that was supposedly all wonderful by giving us Gabe, when really this was just bringing us more and more worry and sadness? And *of course* my mom is *fantastic*. Everybody already knows that. Why should she have to prove it any more than anyone else on the planet?

But there are some thoughts, like the ones I've just mentioned, that you aren't supposed to say out loud because people will think you aren't a very good person. And you certainly aren't supposed to tell someone a lot older than you, especially if she's your gran, that you think she's said something dumb. It's called "respecting your elders." Respecting your elders makes it hard for you to tell the truth about how you feel, especially about so-called important things like God. Or about whether you should be happy or sad about having a retarded brother.

If you want people to believe you're a good person, you have to *use discretion* and keep certain particular truths to yourself.

Chapter 22

The first three days of the second camp were way, *way* better than the week before. They had the same special meals and theme days, but in a different order. And no rain! It was so hot we swam twice a day. But there were bazillions of mosquitoes, which meant we sprayed ourselves constantly, especially before campfire. And of course, we sang with Brad, who Mandy and I were now buddies with, since we were the only girls who stayed for a second week. On Monday night he asked me to lead "Where Have All the Flowers Gone?" because I knew all the lyrics.

I was surprised the girls in my cabin were all so nice; completely different from the week before. During the day we liked hanging out together and every night we laughed our heads off in bed. As for Ella, she seemed to connect with us sometimes, other times not so much.

Tanya put up a schedule for us typical girls. (She'd taken a class about "intellectual disabilities" where they said it's better to call the rest of us "typical," not "normal," and that we should try not to say "Downs child," but put the child first, and say "child with Downs.") Anyway, us typical girls would help to be responsible for Ella by being her buddy for two hours. You made sure she stuck with the group and took her to the outhouse. At meals you watched that she filled her tray with all the foods and reminded her to keep eating, so she'd be done on time. You also helped her with crafts.

After a couple of days we started talking to her more like we did everyone else. I stopped noticing all the strange things, and I really, really listened when she spoke. Well, you had to, because she was hard to understand. Sometimes we were surprised at what she knew, like when Regan caught a garter snake. All the typical girls squealed, but Ella petted it and said, "I like rebtiles."

I was her buddy when we made praying hands. They did the same demonstration as before, but Ella zoned out, maybe because we were sitting too far away. I led her to the demonstration table by the hand. It was so soft, kind of limp, like she didn't have a lot of muscles. I showed her the plaster hands and then she really seemed to get it.

"Ah, pay to Gob," she smiled. She put her hands together like the ornament. "Now I lay me dow to sleep I pay the Lor my so to keep."

"That's it Ella. Praying." And then, out of curiosity I asked, "Who is God, Ella?"

"Gob is my frenn who libs in heaben and gibs pesents."

"Pesents? Oh, presents?"

"Yes. Mom says I am a git fum Gob and Gob gibs da bes pesents."

There was no point telling her "Gob" didn't exist, so therefore she could not be a "git fum Gob." (Churchy people were always saying how everything was a gift. Except for all the bad stuff, of course. Somehow all the bad stuff wasn't from God, and if it was, you were just supposed to forgive God for ruining your life.)

We picked up Ella's supplies and went back to our places. (I didn't take supplies; one set of praying hands was more than enough for a girl who no longer prays.) Ella put her hands together in prayer again, bowed her head, then suddenly said to me, "Look." She opened her hands like a book. "See?"

I didn't see, so she drew a line across her palm with a finger. Then I remembered Gabe, how Mom had shown me his palms. Typical people have two main creases on each palm that don't join together, but a person with Downs has one like that and the other hand has just one continuous crease line. Ella was showing me hers.

I ran my finger across it and nodded. Then she took my hands and followed the creases with her fingers. She looked at me and shrugged, like it was too bad I didn't have a line like hers.

She picked up the plaster and stirred it into the water. I helped her squish the lumps with a spoon. She was extremely picky and wouldn't let me pour the plaster until it was absolutely perfectly smooth. Finally we poured it into the mold and she ran her spatula over the surface forever until it was perfect. When I went to push the wire hook into it she totally freaked. "No! No! Bad!" she screamed and the room went quiet. Everyone gawked at us. Embarrassing or what?

"It's okay Ella," I hissed, "it's just so you can hang it up later."

"Nooooo!" she yelled again.

"Okay, okay, no hook then." I set the wire down, only to have it picked up by Lori.

"I can help," she said, putting her arm around Ella.

And that's when Bizarre Event Number Six happened: another green-gold halo. It shimmered around Lori and Ella, but they seemed totally oblivious to it. I looked around but no one who was looking my way seemed to notice it. I couldn't resist. I reached out my hand and touched Ella's. The halo immediately shot up my arm, down my body, and to my toes. For a few moments I was terrified, but I couldn't pull my hand away. I glanced up at the other two, expecting them to be looking for my reaction, but they were still focused on getting the wire into the plaster. Suddenly, I felt the fear slip away and I went completely calm inside. I closed my eyes. *Everything will be fine. Remember the circle. Everything will be fine.*

The next thing I knew I was crashing to the floor, and when I opened my eyes, Tanya's and several other faces were staring down at me.

"I'm not feeling so good," I said to her and she put her hand on my forehead. She sent Patti running for the nurse. I couldn't see Ella or Lori. I tried to get up, but Tanya kept me down, her hands on my arms. "You shouldn't move," she said. "We don't know what's wrong with you."

"Let me up," I said, "I need to see something." I shook her off me and stood up, wobbling a little. She put her arm around my shoulders to steady me. Lori and Ella were nowhere to be seen. What was going on?

I let Tanya guide me outside onto the front steps of the Gathering Hall. And just as I was beginning to feel like myself again, I witnessed something that only made me feel much, much worse.

Chapter 23

The morning after the police brought me home, I woke up feeling terrible. I snuck downstairs to get breakfast, but stopped at the doorway, surprised to find Dad already up and at the computer. He didn't look like my old dad at all.

"Hi," he said, his eyes dead.

"Hi."

He looked back at the screen. "I'm surfing for stuff on Downs."

"Oh...find anything?"

"Lots...lots and lots."

"Can I make coffee?" I did this sometimes, but usually took it to my parents in bed.

"Sure. Thanks."

Once it was started, I went and looked over his shoulder. He was on a website headed "Pediatric Heart Surgery."

"I've bookmarked some other pages you should read, Shan."

"Okay," I said. This was good. He was focused on Gabriel again. My quasi-arrest was behind us. Even last night, after being at the hospital, it wasn't mentioned. He just sent me to bed.

"What do you want to do today?" he asked and swivelled his chair.

"Besides seeing Gabriel?" He nodded. "I should go to Mandy's and tell her about him before someone else does."

"What'll you say?"

"That he's got the Downs disease."

"It's called a syndrome, Shan. He's got certain conditions that make up a syndrome."

"But Gabe's sick."

"Temporarily."

"He'll always be retarded."

Dad sat up, like it was new information. Then he

sighed and nodded. "But that's not an illness. That's just going to be part of who he is."

"I suppose."

He got up to pour some coffee. "And sweetie, there's a better word than *retarded*. Most websites seem to use *intellectually disabled*. And before you see Mandy, read some of those sites. Then you can tell her about Gabriel in a more informed way."

Talking to Mandy "in a more informed way" appealed to me.

"Now," he said, handing me a scrap of paper with an address, "about the incident at the mall. Two things will happen." My heart fell. "The first is you'll write a letter of apology to the store owner. An apology without any excuses." I felt my eyebrows shoot up to my forehead. "Second, soon you and I will visit that store and you'll hand your letter to the gentleman, and you'll apologize."

"Wha...?"

"Not a word, young lady. The computer's yours. I want the letter before we leave at one-thirty." He opened the door to the backyard saying, just as he left, "Oh, and we *will* be telling Mom about this, but not until she's herself."

I was stunned. Telling Mom and writing a letter was one thing. But the whole idea of seeing Leo again was another. It made me feel completely barfy. I couldn't face breakfast. I sat at the computer and my exceedingly empty brain ached. I typed in the address, just to get myself going. I played around with different fonts for an hour and finally picked one that looked super-cheerful. And then, very slowly, I wrote, and rewrote, the letter until I came up with:

Mr. Leo Sanders
Music Mania Ltd.
#34 – Market Mall
Saskatoon, SK

Dear Mr. Sanders:
Hello. This is Shannon James. I am the person you met last Thursday. In case you don't remember, I am the one who carried one of your CDs out of the store without telling you.

How have you been? I hope you and your family are fine. Things around here are okay. We are extra busy because my mom had a baby named Gabriel and they are still in the hospital. Saylavee!

Anyway, my dad says I should write to you to say I am sorry for taking the CD. It was definitely the most major mistake in my life where I experienced an error in judgment which my dad says I won't repeat because we don't ever want me to go to jail. And I agree totally with him!

So I am sorry for putting the CD under my shirt and everything. I didn't mean to do it, exactly. My dad says I'm not supposed to make up excuses in this letter, but I think I should at least be allowed to say why a person might do the thing I did. I should at least be able to tell you that I am not normally the type to put things under my shirt like that. I have read a very interesting adult book by Dianne Wimsworth and I believe I was possibly having what she calls a Crisis Day. Like I said, things have been a bit crazy around here, what with the baby and other related things that will sound like excuses so I won't list them.

Well, I must go and get ready to go to the hospital.

Hope you have a great day!!!!!!

Warmest regards,
Shannon James

I signed it and gave it to Dad, who was in the back-yard pulling weeds. He stuffed it in his pants pocket without reading it. For a while I helped him weed, but he was intensely silent, and when the phone rang I was happy to run in and get it. It was Mandy, asking for the billionth time: "When do I get to meet Gabriel?"

"In two or three weeks."

"Aw, I'll be at Camp Outlook then," she said, sound-ing genuinely disappointed. When I said, "Can I see you after supper? I've got something to tell you," I heard my voice crack. Mandy heard it too and said, "Shan…what's wrong?"

"I'll tell you tonight. Gotta go. Bye!"

I ran up to my room, lay on my bed, annoyed that I still didn't have my own cell phone like Mandy. If I could have sent her a text she would never have heard the sadness in my voice. I reached to my bedside table and picked up a calendar they'd given us at the hospital. It was from a Down syndrome organization. It was filled with pictures of kids who looked something like Gabriel. Some of the babies stuck their tongues out just like him.

I pictured how Mandy might react to the news. I imagined what exactly I'd tell her, and where I'd *use discretion* because sometimes there are certain particu-lar things a person can think that'll make that person feel a little ashamed later on. Like, for example, what I said about not wanting people to see me in public with Gabriel. That's the kind of thing you should keep to yourself. Then, when you grow up, you're the one, and only one, who can be a little ashamed of your own self.

Chapter 24

Outside the Gathering Hall, as I leaned on Tanya to keep from keeling over, straight ahead at a distance was Brad, walking out of the Mess Hall. He only ever showed up for campfires – what was he doing here now? At the same time, returning from swimming and walking noisily across the Bowl, was my old counselor, Sam, and her girls. She wore a bikini top that was way too small and her towel was wrapped tight and low on her hips so you could see her belly-button ring. The next thing I knew she was veering toward him, waving and going "Brad! Braaaad!" He veered toward her and bang! They were practically chest to chest, yakking. It was disgusting, her being as good as naked and everything. My stomach lurched.

Way over on the other side of them a screen door slammed as Patti and the nurse left her special cabin where they put you if you need stitches or you're the really-barfing-non-stop kind of sick. It took me two seconds to decide what to do. I shook Tanya off me and stumbled down the stairs calling, "Nurse! Nurse!" When Brad turned towards me I took another step, crumpled at the knees, flopped down onto the prickly grass and closed my eyes. Unfortunately, my thigh landed on a thistle, which was supreme torture for a few seconds, until I heard Brad's voice saying my name. He squeezed my shoulder gently and I fluttered my eyelids, like I was surprised and shocked to find myself lying on the ground.

"You okay?" Behind him Tanya's face peered down at me, then Sam's and soon after, the nurse's. She put one hand on my forehead, the other on my wrist to check my pulse saying, "Are you nauseous?" I nodded.

The next thing I knew, Brad was helping me up and guiding my arm around his waist (*around his waist!!!!*) to steady my walk. His back was very bony and he was sweaty from the heat. I caught a faint whiff of the nice smell I remembered from his hanky. I put my other arm around the nurse's plump middle and the three of us moved slowly toward her cabin. I completely forgot about the thistle sticking out of my thigh.

Okay, so the whole fainting thing was a lame girly-girl thing to do, but it worked. Sam disappeared, and I got Brad.

"Don't you usually arrive after supper?" I began, trying to sound weak.

"The boys' camp is next week. I've got extra prep, but oddly enough, I was just about to go looking for you," he said, which made my heart take a good whack at my rib cage.

"Oh?"

"I have a new song for tonight with a cool arrangement for two groups, so I need someone to lead the other part, but since you're not feeling so well…"

"Oh, but I'm sure by tonight I'll be fine," I said, sounding a little too healthy. The nurse opened her cabin door and they shuffled me over to the cot and laid me down. I gazed up into Brad's face as he said, "Well, we'll see. If you're up to a rehearsal later, come find me in the Mess Hall during Free Time. We'll probably need an hour, so be sure your counselor knows where you are."

"Okay, that'd be great!" I resisted the urge to leap up and jump around like a maniac. "I'm already feeling better."

On his way out the door he looked back at me and said, "Then it's a date."

Date? I was too stunned to come up with a cool reply, so I just lay there looking stupid. The nurse stuck a thermometer in my mouth and I happily closed my eyes and imagined everything that might possibly happen during our *date*.

Date! Date! Date!

All right, so I knew it wasn't a date. I'd never actually been on a date. He was joking around, but still...

Date! Date! DATE!

The nurse yanked the thistles out of my leg with her tweezers and I recovered miraculously quickly. All day I looked at my watch every other minute; I thought I would die. Considering what I'd just been through with Lori and Ella, you'd think I'd be busy wondering about my sanity, but instead I was thinking about meeting up with Brad. Goes to show what a little boy attention will do for you.

At long last it was Free Time.

The only other people in the Mess Hall were Mrs. Gormley and the other cooks. Brad moved us to the far corner table so we'd have some privacy. It was very hard to look at him because of the itchy armpit thing. He handed me some music sheets and they trembled in my hands. Mercifully he missed this because at that same moment he reached for his guitar. I rested my arms on the table and read the title.

"Seek and Ye Shall Find."

Oh, great.

During campfires I'd been singing along with the religious songs so people wouldn't guess I was an atheist. But this song was different.

"You know it?" he asked with tons of enthusiasm. I nodded. "Terrific. Then it'll be easy." He began to sing, *"Seek, and ye shall find; Knock and the door will open; Ask, and it shall be given and the love comes a tumbling down…* So why don't you sing that much with me and then I'll show you your part."

I went along with it. I did my best, musically speaking. Part of me couldn't believe I was getting to sing with Beautiful Brad (which was the new nickname this set of campers had bestowed upon him), and part of me kept looking at him and thinking that he seemed too happy and a little bit dumb. It was the way he sang at me with a big grin on his face, like he was entertaining a two-year-old, that finally got me. He wanted me to smile myself silly, looking like I was having a great time, when really the words were stupid, and in my case, a lie.

"You okay, Shan?" he asked, after we'd sung it a dozen times.

"Sure."

"Are you still feeling sick?"

I shook my head.

"Okay." He put down his guitar. "It just seems you aren't really into it."

I focused on a jam blob stuck to the table. All I could think of was how often I'd seen my parents cry in recent years, and how their sadness had stolen something from me. From us. We'd knocked and the door had not been opened. We'd asked and asked and did not get what we'd wanted. What love tumbling down? Give me a break.

"This song is a lie." I heard the words as though they were coming from someone sitting next to me. "This song is a lie, and it's wrong to keep telling people to believe in something that isn't true."

I looked up at him and saw shock and amazement all over his face. I stood up to go.

"Wait," he said. "Why's it a lie?"

"Because God would always have to have compassion to always answer your prayers, and God does not always have compassion. Not for everyone. And since I don't actually believe in God anymore, even telling you this is useless. I guess all I'm saying is I can't sing this song tonight. I'm sorry."

And with that I ran back to my cabin and threw myself on my bunk, my heart thumping so hard I wrapped my arms across my chest to shush it. Technically, I wasn't supposed to be there if my counselor wasn't. Whatever. What could they do anyway? Send me home? Like that'd be a bad thing.

For the first time in a week I wanted to get out, to leave Camp Outlook behind and go home, but not to the empty home I'd left. I wanted to see my mom and dad waiting at the door with huge laughing smiles on their faces, then run inside to the crib where baby Gabriel would be cooing and smiling up at me with normal eyes and his tongue not sticking out.

It was really very simple: when it came to having a brand-new baby in my family, all I wanted was to feel complete, total, supreme, pure, happiness.

That.

Was.

All.

Chapter 25

"Were you offered prenatal testing?" the doctor asked my mom. He was new to me, but was dressed in a lab coat and holding a clipboard like all the rest.

"We turned it down," she replied, "didn't want to risk another miscarriage." He scribbled a note. She flipped through a form he'd handed her. They needed to know if Gabe got Downs because of her old age or because of something in our family's genes. He left her with a pen, and a lot of stress. The questions caused her to sigh heavily, or hiss things like, "How would I know that?" or "What woman keeps track of this stuff?" She wrote ferociously.

Dad had been right: this was not the time to tell her that the cops had been around for a visit.

While all this was going on, I'd been cuddling my sleeping brother. The tip of his tiny pink tongue rested between his lips. He stirred, then gave the cutest yawn and squeak. My heart twisted with love and I was so glad for the aching of it; that it had come even though I knew he had Downs. I'd been afraid that all the anger inside me would make loving Gabe impossible.

I touched his miniscule fingers, compared them to the chapped hands of the man at the mall. Bizarrely, Gabe would be a man one day, a grown person out doing whatever in the world.

Would I love him then?

He would still need us, Mom, Dad, me, in order to survive. We would be responsible for his life. Then it hit me: maybe in ten years my parents would die in a car accident and I'd be *totally* responsible for Gabe for the whole rest of my life. This was the first of many times I imagined this Mom-and-Dad-Dying scenario, which always caused a huge horribleness to come over me that was hard to get rid of.

Mom touched my arm and gave me a start. I'd been thinking way too hard and my head hurt.

"Nice to hold him, eh, Shan?"

She reached for him. She was still in a wheelchair, so I got up and moved her closer to the bassinette so Gabe's tubes and wires didn't get stretched.

Nurses were everywhere in the Neonatal Unit, trying to make sure all the tiny babies stayed alive. Gabe's nurse came over. She was tall and black, and, like everyone else, she wore a hairnet.

"How's our little peanut doing?" She smiled at Gabe like she was in love with him too.

"We're going to attempt this again," Mom said, putting Gabe to her breast.

"Good for you, Mom. It's so important he get the real thing," said the nurse. "Now honey, you just take your time and call if you need me."

When she'd left Mom whispered, "She's one of the helpful ones. This morning's nurse gave me two minutes to get him to latch on and then began badgering me to give him formula. Unbelievable."

She spoke softly to him, begged him to open his mouth, and suddenly went, "Hey, that's it Gabe! Atta boy! He did it Shan – he finally latched properly!"

To my surprise, she began crying. It was a bigger deal than I'd thought. And it was the happiest I'd seen her in two days. Gabe only sucked for five minutes but the nurse agreed that was an excellent start, and he'd get a little formula as well, just to fill his tummy.

I wheeled Mom to meet up with Dad, sitting in the waiting room, and he looked relieved when we told him about Gabe latching on. Even though Mom still looked horrible, what with being all swollen up and no make-up and flat hair and her bag of pee still hanging off the side of her chair, Dad leaned toward her, took her two hands in his, and said, "You are the most beautiful woman in the world."

✝✝✝

Later, after supper, I walked the three blocks to Mandy's, thinking about what to tell her and what not to tell her. I would never, in a billion years, tell her about the cops bringing me home. Don't think I wasn't tempted because I'd love to have seen the look on her face, but my life would definitely have been ruined. So, I decided I'd tell her only about Gabriel. That'd be shocking enough.

Mrs. Gormley met me at the door.

"Congratulations Shannon!" she bubbled. "We're so thrilled for your family!" She threw her arms around me. "How are Mom and Baby?"

"They're great, thanks." I tried to be as enthusiastic as she was.

"Well, after your call this morning, we've been a little worried."

Jeesh. Mandy'd already blabbed about the one tiny hint I'd given her on the phone. I ignored the question.

"Where is she?"

Mrs. Gormley gave me a funny look. "Downstairs."

I found her at the computer surrounded by stacks of papers and boxes of junk the Gormleys had collected. I swept my arm across the couch to clear it and flopped down.

"Hi," she said, focused on the screen where an alien was blowing up.

"Why'd you tell your mom something was wrong?"

She swivelled her chair around. "You didn't say it was a big secret. I don't even know what *it* is." I rolled my eyes and she rolled herself over on the chair. "You bring pictures?"

"No. My dad hasn't downloaded them yet."

We sat silent for a moment.

"So?" She raised her eyebrows.

I couldn't make the words come out. I didn't want her to see me be sad about Gabe. I wanted to be strong for him. I wanted people to be happy he was on the planet. I swallowed hard and said it out loud without croaking. "My brother has Down syndrome."

And there it was, the look on her face that I'd been imagining. I had truly shocked and amazed her. I'd thought I'd feel *something*, at least some sort of glee that I, for once, had an incredible piece of news for her. But I just felt numb.

Mandy sat there, speechless. Finally she said, "That's too bad."

"But he's actually very cute. Very beautiful, even," I replied. "I'll email a picture. You'll see."

Her eyes brimmed with tears, which made me weepy too. She wiped her cheeks and swivelled her chair back and forth for a minute. "How are your parents?"

"They aren't exactly thrilled."

In the end, Mandy and I didn't talk much about the situation, so she didn't get to hear me talk about it "in a more informed way." For some reason that didn't seem to matter. We played a game, watched some TV, and then I left.

When I stepped into the house my dad was on the phone.

"A casserole would be wonderful," I heard him say. "Thanks for your concern.... Yes, it certainly was unexpected.... Yes. Thank you. Yes. Wonderful. Good-bye, Denise."

Denise. Denise Gormley. As in *Mrs.* Gormley.

It had taken me all of five minutes to walk home.

Chapter 26

If Mandy weren't Mandy two things could've happened:
1) Instead of lying on my bunk in a huff, I could've gone and found her and told her what'd just happened with Brad wanting to sing a song with me, and 2) In carrying out #1, I could have also been honest and told Mandy I was actually an atheist and why. BUT, Mandy being Mandy, she would for sure blab about the atheist thing to *someone*, making life at a church camp a tiny bit awkward.

So, I lay there, torturing myself by recalling the look on Brad's face when I told him the truth about things. Why did I feel guilty?

I still liked him. A lot. It wasn't just that he was a hottie. He had been nice to me. I loved the way he talked, and sang, and played guitar. Would it be *so* bad to sing about something you didn't believe in?

Maybe.

Probably.

Even if I changed my mind, I was too chicken to face him. What if he asked me questions I didn't want to answer? *Couldn't* answer.

I rolled onto my side and saw Ella's stuff, which immediately reminded me of Bizarre Event #6. How could I have forgotten it? Just hours ago, I was lying on the floor having truly fainted. I'd never fainted before in my life. And that glowing business had been no trick of the eye. I'd seen it on my own body, for heaven's sake. Is this what was meant when someone said you were hallucinating? Did crazy murderers see this kind of thing before they axed someone? Inside my gut a huge knot was developing.

I counted the days at camp so far: ten. Six bizarre events in ten days! And I was starting to lose track of what they were.

I grabbed my autograph book from the bunk shelf and began to write them all down on the back pages:

The Bizarre Events Of Camp Outlook
As Witnessed By Shannon B. James

- Thought I heard Bonnie say <u>Baby Gabriel</u>

- Lori gave me a funny feeling / she said something like everything will be fine and that I was lucky to be in the circle

- Lori calmed Bonnie and hugged her and they glowed outside Mandy's cabin

- At campfire Lori was sitting way across from me, but her voice popped into my ear like she was right next to me and said <u>You are part of the circle</u>

- At another campfire I heard voices singing in my head repeating <u>It belongs to all of us</u> / looked at Ella / she mouthed those exact words in time with the voice in my head!!

- Lori helped Ella with her craft and put her arm around her / <u>they</u> did the glow thing, then when I touched them, <u>I did it too!!!!!</u>

I read over the list several times and a chill crept down my spine. It was definitely adding up to me being totally crazy. Add to that the CD thing at the store, and mentally I was not looking good at all. And there was one other noticeable thing: Lori was part of four of the six events. Why?

In the distance there were shrieks and laughter. Campers were returning from the pool. I set my book on the shelf and ran outside to see Patti and Ella racing toward me, towels flying off their shoulders like superheroes.

Patti let Ella touch the porch first. "Hey Shannon," she grinned. "I'm the one! I win! I win!" She laughed and laughed.

"Right on, Ella," I said. "That was awesome!" Deep down inside of me I could feel that I meant it, too. I wasn't just being nice to her. There *was* something awesome about her, about her kind of happiness. When she threw her arms around me and hugged me for too long, I let her. And I looked at my arms while she did. No sign of any green-glow. Why not now?

"You feel good?" she said.

"I'm fine," I replied.

"Good," she said and went running into the cabin.

Just before supper I called my parents on Mrs. Gormley's cell. They put me on speaker so they could keep eating; Mom had to get back to the hospital to feed

Gabe at an exact time. I'd called once earlier that week, so they already knew about Ella and how she looked like Gabe's sister more than I did. I told them about Ella winning the race, how I'd been in charge of her at the pool the day before. She'd worn water wings and been very intense about her swimming lesson, like she was totally loving the experience. It'd been kind of humorous to watch, but in a celebration way, not a making-fun-of-her kind of way.

After I'd blabbed all this out, there was a pause.

"It's good you've met Ella," Mom finally said. She sounded tired. She'd been sleeping at the hospital so she could feed Gabriel during the night. The good news was, he was nursing much better, so he might be home by the time camp was over.

"Cross your fingers," said Dad. And from then on I did, every time I pictured Gabe. My fingers and my toes.

Which is what I was doing later at the campfire when Brad arrived, crossing everything including my legs and arms. I pretended to be talking intensely with Patti, but when he started singing, eventually our eyes met. He winked at me, and did *not* make all of us sing "Seek and Ye Shall Find."

Chapter 27

In the afternoon the day after I'd told Mandy about Gabe, the doorbell rang. She and her mom were on our doorstep with a chicken casserole, salad, homemade buns, chocolate cake, and a gift for my brother: a puzzle to teach him about shapes and colors.

It was stinking hot again, so Dad asked them in for lemonade. Dad still wasn't his old self, but he tried hard to be a good host. After he'd told them all about the Neonatal Unit, he opened his laptop and showed them photos.

"He's a darling, an absolute angel. You chose a perfect name," Mrs. Gormley said, gushily. "But how are you and Nora coping?"

"We're hangin' in there," he replied. "I've never had so many conflicting emotions."

"I'm sure I can't imagine." She patted Dad's knee, which was nice of her, but then she said, "Just remember Darryl – God knew you'd be the best possible parents for Gabriel or He wouldn't have sent him to you."

I bit my tongue. Like my gran, she was completely forgetting Gabe wasn't the baby we'd wanted. And I know Dad didn't agree with her either, because some weeks later I heard him say to Mom, "I wish people'd stop acting like God keeps a list of saintly parents who'd be perfect for all the Downs kids. What about the parents who give theirs away? What's that then? God screwing up?"

With Mrs. Gormley, though, Dad was too polite to argue.

"Now, Darryl," she went on, "I've been thinking… why don't you send Shannon to our house when you need to be at the hospital. For meals, overnight, whatever helps."

Mandy and I glanced at one another with wide eyes and big smiles. Then I had a worry.

"But Dad," I said, "I'd still get to visit the baby, right?"

"Yes, of course," he said, "and thanks so much

Denise. I do have some work to finish before I can start my paternity leave."

"No problem," she replied, and then he gave me a certain particular look and added, "Even though she's almost a teenager, it seems Shannon isn't old enough to be left alone."

Puh-*lease*. In front of my best friend? I rolled my eyes at Mandy, who didn't know what the heck my dad was talking about. Mrs. Gormley smiled weirdly as she stood up because she didn't get it either. "I'm sure she'll be fine with us."

"Yes, of course," he said. "I'll run it by Nora and call you."

"Whatever we can do." She picked up her purse at the door. "Oh, and one more thought. If Gabriel's in the hospital beyond next week, we'd love it if Shannon would come to Camp Outlook with us. It's less than an hour from here. A church camp. There's still room for more."

"But I have to be here when my brother comes home," I blurted. "It'd be totally impossible for me to go."

"Thanks Denise," replied Dad, "but I'm hopeful we'll have our baby home before then."

I breathed a great sigh of relief.

Chapter 28

Because of the rain during the first week of camp, none of us got to sleep under the stars. But this week, by Wednesday, everything had dried up enough to do so. After campfire, three cabins of girls took their turns sleeping on Crocus Hill.

The next morning at breakfast they were all abuzz. They'd seen shooting stars! Lots of them! Even though the moon had been full and washed out some of the sky. My cabin and two others would sleep outdoors next. We could hardly wait for the day to end.

Before vespers we had everything packed: extra sweatshirts, socks, sleeping bags, bug spray. After the sing-along, returning to the Bowl, we were well ahead of everyone else. We couldn't get our backpacks on fast enough. Ella looked confused.

"Time for bed!" she reminded us.

"Yes," I tried to explain, "we're going to bed. But up on the hill!" She cocked her head and I took her by the hand.

As we walked toward it, even with thirty flashlights glowing, she still held one hand over her eyes so she didn't have to see the dark. This really slowed us down, especially on the narrow path from the Bowl through the bush. Coyotes howled in the distance and some of the girls shrieked. Ella howled back and laughed, her hand still covering her eyes.

The moon was full and bright, so it was easy to find the sloping trail to the top. It wasn't much of a hill, really; more like a pimple. I'd already been partway up on a nature hike the week before. Without going to the top, we'd still been able to see for miles. The prairie was that flat.

This time we crossed right over the top of the hill and found a kind of plateau area, surrounded by low, spotty brush. There were three small fire pits lined with stones.

"Okay girls," barked Tanya, "unroll your sleeping bags around the pits."

"But not too close," warned Sam. She wore a giant sparkly clip in her hair and long earrings that flashed in the moonlight. Hardly camp wear, but whatever.

Once our bags were laid out like flower petals around each pit, and the fires were blazing, we crawled into our bags, feet to the fire. I was near the outside edge of the plateau, between Ella and Regan. Ella seemed calm, but she still had a hand over her eyes and refused to look at the stars. I reached over and took her other hand from on top of her sleeping bag and held it.

"Ella...Ella, look at me." She rolled her head toward mine and lifted her fingers just enough to see me. "Ella, you don't need to be frightened. Don't you want to see the stars?"

She rolled back and put *both* hands over her eyes, so I gave up.

Sam was lying a few feet away from me, her head just inches from mine. The idea of our two brains lying so close together, thinking about the same boy, irritated me no end. So I tried extra hard not to think about Brad, or Sam, or him and her together, and stared up into the night, listening to everyone *oooo* and *aaaah* over the incredible star-studded sky.

I'd never slept under the stars. In the city you just see the brightest ones. But here you got the real picture, the whole picture. Every tiny, precious glittering star that belonged to the universe.

I pressed the light on my watch; almost eleven. Someone squealed, "Hey! Did you see that?" and others shouted, "What? Where?"

"A falling star, just over there!"

"Where?"

"There, where I'm pointing. Near the Big Dipper."

"Where's the Big Dipper?"

"Right there! Look toward the moon!"

"Where?"

And that's how it went for a while, till we heard a vehicle in the distance. We gradually stopped talking. Soon headlights were bouncing along the dirt road leading to the hill. It screeched to a stop just at the bottom and a guy hollered, "Over here! Go this way!"

In the firelight our eyes grew huge and some girls began bursting with extremely girly giggles. When the doors slammed shut the girls just got louder and sillier until Shelley shouted, "That's enough! Settle down, please! We counselors will deal with it."

Then more shrieks, more giggles, like it was a big joke. Some, like me, were getting nervous. Ella had finally taken her hands off her eyes and looked confused again.

"Oh fer cryin' out loud, y'all," yelled Sam. "Shee-ut the hal up right quick, puh-lease and thank ya!" And finally everyone did. In silence we listened to the sounds of tramping feet and breaking branches as they got closer and closer.

The counselors shone their flashlights toward the noise and finally Tanya went, "Hello? Hello-o-o-o? Who's there, please?"

The beams caught the faces of three guys who shielded their eyes from the light as they climbed up onto the plateau. They were maybe twenty, wearing jean jackets and cowboy boots (as well as jeans and T-shirts, of course). Each had a beer. (This means they'd probably been drinking and driving – an extremely bad thing to do.) A bunch of campers suddenly shrieked and giggled, making the guys laugh in an embarrassed way till one said, "Oops, Girl Guides. Not what we were looking for...."

Another said, "Jailbait City, boys," which made no sense, and then, "Hey, could ya please quit with the interrogation lights?"

Gradually each counselor lowered her flashlight. Now the guys could see it wasn't just all "tween" girls up here; they just stood there looking gaga. All three counselors were really pretty, not to mention Sam's obvious resemblance to Britney Spears.

"Well, hi," said the guys.

"Hi," said the counselors. There was a long pause, then Tanya said, "Can we help you?"

They snorted a laugh. "That depends," said the one who hadn't talked yet. The next thing we knew the counselors and the guys (who were really quite loud – my mom would've called them obnoxious) were into a big enthusiastic chit-chat about what people around Outlook did for a good time, and why the counselors had come to work at the camp, and where they'd come from originally. Of course, when the guys heard Sam's Texan accent, they were all impressed and made fun of her in a kind of way that actually meant they liked her a lot. Right before our eyes, Sam and Shelley turned from bossy mother-types into soft, smiley-faced-girly-girl-types, flipping their hair and swaying back and forth as they talked. Tanya didn't seem quite so impressed, and several times she was the one who reminded the other two that it was time to settle us girls and get us to sleep. We looked on, an audience of twenty-five at a play, wondering what would happen next.

"You girls wanna beer?" the cutest one asked. (They were all hotties though, which my cabinmates and I agreed about later.)

"No thank you," said Tanya, grabbing the hands of the other two and pulling them, backwards, toward our campfires.

"Nice meeting you," said Sam, and you could tell by the way she said it that if it weren't for us, she would've taken a beer in a flash.

"Well, if you change your minds," the ultra-cute one said, "we'll be camping just down there in the truck." As they left he turned back.

"Hey Texas, what did ya say your name was again?"

"I didn't," she said, smiling in a teasy kind of way.

"No problem," he said, "I'll just call ya Texas." As he made his way down the hill he cried, "Texas! Texas! Oh, Texas! Oh, Tex-*aaaassss!*" That made us all laugh, since Sam often exposed most of hers in her super-low-cut jeans.

Then we campers had to discuss every detail about what had just happened, as if we hadn't all witnessed exactly the same thing. Our counselors tried to turn back into our mothers, but we'd seen their girly side so it was much easier to ignore them. Even though Tanya had acted all responsible and whatnot, she still couldn't stop smiling. Regan mimicked the way they'd behaved, wiggling her hips and flipping her hair, and soon we were killing ourselves. The counselors tried to look mad, but couldn't because they were all glowy due to having just had major boy-attention.

By twelve-thirty Ella was snoring deeply and just a couple of girls were awake, whispering. Eventually they stopped and I felt very alone. I pondered the patterns of the stars, made a game of inventing constellations. And that's when I saw my first-ever shooting star, just below the moon, and low in the sky. Then there was another! And another!

I checked my watch again. One-thirty. I considered waking everybody, but then the stars stopped falling. So I closed my eyes and began to feel every lump in the ground. I shuffled over a couple of feet toward Ella to a smoother spot. A few feet away the plateau sloped gently down to the open prairie.

I was almost asleep when, from the direction of the slope, I heard something move in the grass. I completely and totally froze, picturing a coyote poised, ready to clamp its jaws around my throat. Another rustle. I wanted to shout a warning, but what if the noise brought on the attack? I played dead. The rustling went on and on as the coyote chose its victim. My chest thudded so loud I was certain the beast could hear it and would pick me.

And then I couldn't believe my ears.

"Hey, Texas," a voice whispered, "*Texa-a-a-as!*"

Oh, great. And he was probably totally blotto by now.

"*Texa-a-a-as!*"

"Sh!" I heard Sam crawling out of her sleeping bag. "I'm coming!"

Then they were both rustling the grass. I turned my head very slowly and watched the ultra-cute guy, just a short distance from me, take her hand and help her down the hill. When they were out of sight I sat up. The fires were dead. In the moonlight everyone was sound asleep. I fell back under the starry sky, perplexed about what to do. I rolled onto my side and came face-to-face with Ella's wide-open, saucer eyes, staring at me like a zombie, which gave me a heart attack of another order.

"Ella!" I shout-whispered. "Jeesh, go back to sleep!"

She obeyed and once I heard her snoring, I closed my eyes again, wondering if I should wake up Tanya or Shelley. But Ella began moving around and when I turned to her again, she was gone! I bolted upright just in time to see her heading down the hill, taking the same route Sam had taken. I screamed, "Ella! Ella come back!" but she kept on. The noise should've woken everyone. I yelled after her again, louder. No one moved. She was getting harder to see. By the time I'd yanked on my runners, grabbed my sweater, and started down the hill, she'd disappeared.

Chapter 29

Mrs. Gormley's cooking was delicious. Dad and I completely pigged out. Then he informed me that he'd called the CD store and Leo would be expecting us that evening. We'd stop on the way to the hospital.

"One day when there's more time," he said, "I'll explain the difference between a personal letter and a business letter."

I wasn't so sure what he meant, but whatever. I was glad to not have the explanation just then.

"Further," he went on in his lecturey voice, "having a Crisis Day is no reason for stealing. Your mom and I are having a Crisis Week, and you didn't see us robbing a bank."

Well, thank goodness for that, I thought. *That* would've been totally embarrassing.

At the mall I thought for sure I was going to throw up just before seeing Leo, but in the end it wasn't so awful. Dad made me spend my allowance on flowers and I gave them to Leo with the letter. Then I had to say "sorry" in person. He shook hands with both of us and seemed happy we'd stopped by.

Walking back to the car I said, "So when are you going to tell Mom?"

"I won't be," he replied. I was in the middle of my silent sigh of relief when he went, "You. You will be telling her. After Gabriel's home."

Jeesh. Like I hadn't been through enough already. I stuck my earphones in and refused to talk the whole way to the hospital. I was stressing out about how I'd tell her, what words I'd use, what she'd say, how she'd go ballistic on me, until the moment we walked into her room and found her lying on the bed in tears.

"Something just went wrong," she choked.

Dad hugged her. "What happened?"

"I fed him, put him in the bassinette and then he

coughed a little and the heart thing beeped, but it beeps all the time so I did nothing, but when I looked at him again he was turning blue and his little eyes looked so horrible, his lips stretched tight, so I yelled for the nurse...and...and...the look on her face...she was so scared Darryl."

Mom's breath was caught up in big sobs, and Dad's face went white. Her tears brought on my own, so now Dad had two sobbers to deal with.

"But is he okay, Nora?"

"I don't know. There was a rush of nurses, a couple of doctors. They made me leave. It was minutes ago. I knew you were on your way so I came here to wait for you, to take you there. It's too much Darryl," she said, weeping into his shoulder, and Dad went, "I know, Nora, I know."

"Shan," he said. "Wait here. Someone'll come for you as soon as we know...anything."

I nodded and watched him help Mom out the door. For the first time it entered my head that it'd be an extremely, *extremely,* terrible thing if something happened to our Gabe. Like, for instance, if he should die because of his heart, or anything else you could think of.

It had been just three days since he'd come to us instead of the baby we'd really wanted. It was such a sad and tragic thing. Now I understood it would be much worse if he were to die.

I'd decided I couldn't believe in God, and I knew saying a prayer was a useless way to get what you wanted, but I had to do something.

It maybe sounds weird, but here's what I did: I tried to find all the love I could inside me. In my mind's eye I turned that love into millions of multi-colored speckles, like I'd seen in my dream when I was five. I pictured the speckles swirling around and around until finally I zapped them out of my brain and into the air. I saw them shoot under the door, and my mind's eye followed them through a maze of hallways until they found their way to Gabriel's bassinette, where they covered him like a blanket.

That was all I could think to do, and once I'd done all I could do, I stopped crying.

Chapter 30

I skittered down the hill, zigzagging through shrubs. At any moment I might break my ankle in a gopher hole, but I made it to the bottom in one piece. A ways off was a grove of tall bushes silhouetted against a pale fire. The wood crackled. I recognized Sam's soft laughter; the low tones of the drunk guy. Any second now I would hear their surprised voices as Ella burst in on them.

I waited, panting from my run. I waited some more. This was taking too long. I was just about to yell to Sam when, right behind me, a twig snapped. I spun toward it. Nothing.

Then, several yards over, I caught Ella's moonlit

shape skirting the base of the hill. She seemed to glide along, hands at her sides. *Sleepwalking?*

"Ella-a-a-a! Ella-a-a-a-a-a-a-a!!" She didn't stop.

I screamed up the hill, "Tanya-a-a! Help me! Ella's in trouble!"

No one called back and meanwhile I'd lost sight of her. I ran partway around the hill, caught site of Ella again, got close enough to grab her, but found I was grasping at air. I froze. *What the...?* She'd been right there; right in front of me.

"Oh I wisssss I wuzzzz a wittle ba-a-a-ah a sssoap..." I heard her singing, strangely high and slowly. The song called to me and there she was, quite a distance now from the hill, her figure clearly outline by moonlight against the dark prairie sky. I ran to her, and once again she allowed me to get just close enough, then disappeared, instantly reappearing yards away, her back always to me. *What's going on? Doesn't she see me?* I looked back at Crocus Hill, and considered running up to wake everyone. *"...I would slippeeee and I'd slideeeee o-o-over evereeebodeee's hideeeee..."* The eerie song pulled me, guided me, led me to her over and over as she flashed from one place to the next. Her song changed. *"A-a-all Go-o-od's cri-i-itters go-o-ot a pla-a-ace in the choir, sssso-o-ome sssi-i-ing lo-o-o-ow, sssssssome*

sssssing hi-i-i-igher..." And this is how we traveled for what seemed a very long time and a very long way from Crocus Hill.

Then, under my feet, the earth began to drop, slowly, my shins brushed against shrubs. Soon my knees and thighs were being scratched by higher bushes. My heart raced, sensing I was being swallowed up in a tangle of sharp branches. *"...and ssssome jusssst cla-a-a-ap their ha-a-a-ands..."* I followed her voice and saw that she'd found a narrow path cutting through thick trees. And yet, despite what had quickly become a forest, the moon was always visible. Its rays caught in Ella's hair like a beacon.

She was following it! The whole time she'd been heading straight toward it!

"Ella! Ella come here! I need to talk to you!" I yelled, now running easily along the path. But she wouldn't turn around. I grabbed at her back. *Poof!* Gone again. I stopped, waited for the song. Waited for her to reappear. Nothing.

My head hurt. I started thinking crazy thoughts, remembered the movie *Gone So Long*. What if I was being lured into the forest just so a psycho could kill me? I wanted to go home. I wanted Mom and Dad. I wanted my old life. My life before Gabriel.

A coyote howled at my back and I freaked, sprinted on without thinking, heading straight for the moon. Still no sign of Ella. Soon the trail grew thick with thistles and vines until there was no path at all.

I ripped and slashed, was close to collapse, when a flash of warm light lit up the forest. It flashed again, this time brighter than daylight, its source somewhere ahead. For a few seconds everything was lush and green. Flowers popped here and there. The last glimmer revealed an obvious pathway. I ran into it, told myself I must be running toward a farmyard. The farmer had heard the coyotes and turned on his yard light to scare them off. He'd rescue me, help me find a way back to my parents, as they used to be. Yes, he would.

But there was no farmer, no farmyard.

Instead, the throbbing light became brighter and greener, and the dense jungle gave way to flat open ground between spotty shrubs and trees. Voices were singing, the same tune I'd heard in my head at campfire a few nights earlier, when Ella mouthed the words. I double-freaked, clueless about what to do other than carry on, crawling now on my hands and knees toward the sound. I squeezed my eyes shut. *Wake up! Wake up!!* But the singing just grew louder, the light burned brighter, my heart pounded harder.

I crept up behind tall prairie grass growing along a ledge of earth, terrified to look beyond it.

You must do this. You must save Ella. You have no choice.

I lay right down flat on my belly. Slowly I slipped my hands into the grass and pulled it aside, peeked through. Below me the land dropped steeply, then swept gently down into a depression, as though a large, deep pond had been drained dry. Some fifty feet downhill, the incredible scene in the basin left me wide-eyed and totally petrified.

Chapter 31

Two days after Gabe had turned blue and scared everybody, there was good news and bad news. The bad news was they still weren't sure what had caused it, and he was struggling to stay healthy. They were keeping an eye on his heart, but they didn't think that was the problem. He was too weak to nurse, which upset Mom because he'd been doing so well. She had to pump milk instead, which she hated.

The good news was she got the staples out of her belly. (Picture Frankenstein's monster.) She was less sore, but had to move carefully, so nothing popped open. (Yuck.)

Two more days passed, and there was more good news and bad news. The good news was that Gabe was getting healthier again and had started to nurse. The bad news was my mom had an infection where the staples had been, and even worse, an eye doctor had found cataracts growing in one of Gabe's eyes, so he would need surgery in a few days to remove them. Thankfully, Dad was finally on his leave from work, because my mom was now a complete wreck. I didn't go to the hospital too often anymore, and I was glad because she was hard to look at. Anyway, the nurses wouldn't let me see Gabe while he was so sick.

Up until that day I'd been spending more and more time at Mandy's. Since Dad had told Mrs. Gormley I wasn't allowed to go to the mall, Mandy and I had only one other option if we wanted to run into Rick Santana (me) or Jarad Hughes (Mandy): the skateboard park.

There was a fifty percent chance of seeing them there, and they'd usually talk to us if ultra-cool girls weren't around. If they were, Mandy and I'd find a reason to leave. They had a way of making us feel invisible. Like we didn't count.

But here's the thing about Rick: for the last half of grade seven, I got the feeling I was more than a friend. He would start the conversation. And sometimes he came over to me to do it. A special effort. So sometimes I dared to imagine he would ask me out. Then everyone would know a cool guy had picked me. I even pictured us in a band together, since he played electric guitar. But there were two problems: 1) in a crowd, you only ever saw him with cool, ultra-cool, or very pretty girls, and 2) while I was not a Geek, or abnormal, I was also not cool or pretty. I was an okay, average person.

I did escape being a Geek, and for that I was always thankful. Geeks were not well treated by some of the Cools. In fact, you could say they were treated exceedingly meanly. Even if you just did something special, like my solo in the grade six talent show, they would be mean. They said I sounded like a cat in heat. (I did not enter the grade seven show.)

The problem? Even though Mandy and I didn't like the Cools, when it came to certain particular hotties, there were days we badly wanted to be like them. And it was possible for this to happen as late as grade seven: for example, Sue Morrison. She did it by starting to smoke and getting cigarettes from her brother to pass on to them. Not all the Cools smoked though, so I imagined I could possibly buy them junk food. This would save having to die an ugly poster death from cancer.

Better than buying junk food would be Rick. If he

showed the Cools he liked me, maybe I wouldn't be so invisible. Maybe they'd even say I was a good singer. These were the kinds of thoughts going through my head the day something I don't much like to talk about happened.

It was the Wednesday afternoon, eight days after Gabe was born, and the day *before* I was told I'd be going to Camp Outlook, like it or not. Mandy and I went to the skateboard park, and sure enough, there was Rick, practising with a few others from school. (There was no Jarad for her to ogle.) I followed Mandy up the bleachers to the top and we began nonchalantly tanning.

Soon, as I'd hoped, Rick was climbing up with his skateboard under his arm.

"Hey," he said.

"Hey," Mandy and I replied. Then she moved away, pretended to be sleeping in the sun, just as we'd agreed. He sat next to me and said, "So, you're a big sister now."

Word had traveled fast. Did he know about the Downs?

"Yeah," I said, "his name's Gabriel. He's adorable."

There was an awkward pause. Finally I said, "Do you have a brother?"

"Two sisters in high school."

"Oh. That's nice."

That's nice????? In my mind I rolled my eyes. *Dorky, dorky, dorky.* Just as I was trying to come up with something more interesting to say, there were hoots from the other side of the park. A gang of kids was cutting through the trees and coming our way. Soon I could pick out Al Warner, Sue Morrison, Fiona Stevens, Janice Sweeny, Danny O'Maley, Shawn McNabb, Todd Gronsdahl and the rest of the Cools, a few of them smoking and some carrying boards.

Why now?

Mandy opened her eyes and yelled, "Hi Sue!" When Sue looked up but didn't reply, Mandy closed her eyes again and pretended Sue was deaf.

They hit the ramps and soon there was a lot of showing off and swearing going on, Al Warner being the loudest. He was now super-famous, thanks to Mandy. Among the Cools he was revered for having punched a teacher. Mandy'd told me she heard that next year he'd be going to one of those high schools for kids with "issues," supposedly to keep him from ending up in jail as an adult. Good luck with that.

"I think Al popped too many at lunch," joked Rick. At least I think he was joking. Mercifully the cool girls remained focused on Al, so Rick and I carried on trying to have a conversation. Once we got onto music we found lots to say. He pulled out his iPod and let me use his ear buds so I could hear some of the new songs he'd bought. There were a lot of bands I hadn't heard of and he just kept skimming through them, letting me hear a few seconds of each song. Then I pulled out my iPod and he listened in. We were getting so intense about our favorite bands that we didn't notice what was going on below us, until Mandy looked up and groaned, "Oh, no."

From the bleachers we could see Paul Kordinski and another guy walking along the path that crossed the park and passed next to the ramps. Already hoots had started from some of the skateboarders, but Paul kept his head down, ignoring everyone the same way he did when he pushed Bruce's wheelchair around at school. But when he was with his brother, everyone pretty much left Paul alone.

But he wasn't with his brother now.

"Kordinski!" Al shouted, then pointing at Paul's friend, "Kordinski! Who's yer girlfriend?" The bimbos standing around Al tittered.

Paul walked faster.

"Kordinski!" Shawn McNabb yelled. "We asked you a question. You're s'posed to stop when we talk at ya."

Al slapped Shawn on the back and opened his big fat mouth again. "Hey ugly! My friend here told you to stop!" That was Paul's cue to turn and run like hell back the way he'd come, his friend lagging just behind. Al and his gang of jerks chased them, followed by Sue Morrison and two other girls. A few Cools hung back and began comparing cell phones, as if nothing was going to happen. As Mom would say, they were in denial.

We all jumped to our feet and Rick took the bleachers down two at a time and took off across the grass. Mandy and I followed, but lost sight of everyone for a minute. We rounded a grove of trees and found them all in a big circle around Al Warner, who had Paul Kordinski by the scruff of the neck so his T-shirt cut into his armpits. He was terrified, his nose bloodied. He tried to shake himself loose, but Al was a foot taller and stronger than him. Paul's puny friend stood a good distance away, rocking back and forth, torn between running and helping. Rick paced outside the circle sizing up the situation, fear all over his face.

"We've been through this before, Kordinski," Al sneered. "When you're told to stop, you stop."

He slammed his fist under Paul's rib cage and I gasped. I was scared out of my wits for him, remembering how Al had smashed my back against the school wall.

Paul glanced at me with pleading eyes. I will never, ever forget that.

Al said to everybody, "So, what d'you guys have to say to him?"

"You're a worthless piece of shit, Kor–stink–ski," yelled Todd Gronsdahl.

"Garbage, like you doesn't deserve to live!" hissed Janice Sweeny.

"After we're done pounding the hell out of you, we're going after your faggot friend," hollered Danny O'Maley. The friend ran. Wise choice.

Finally, Sue Morrison took the parting shot.

"You and that retard brother of yours must be twins!"

My heart stopped. I couldn't believe my ears.

But she had barely two seconds to look around for approval because Paul went totally and completely ballistic. He broke away from Al like a super-hero, firing himself head first straight at Sue's stomach. He smashed her to the ground screaming so loud you couldn't understand him. He was smart enough not to sit on her too long and bounded up again, slashing his way through the circle of stunned creeps. He was gone before they knew what had happened.

No sooner had Paul taken off than Mandy left my side and was over helping Sue to her feet, saying, "You okay, Sue? You okay?" Her whole body had hit the ground hard, so she was shaken and crying. "Can you believe that asshole?" she said.

"I know, I know," Mandy replied.

I spun around and marched away from it all as fast as I could. At the edge of the park I could hear her shouting after me to wait. I wiped my nose with the bottom of my shirt and kept walking, but soon she was at my heels. We didn't speak till the top of my street when she said, "That was pretty awful, eh Shan?"

"Yep."

"What a bunch of total jerks they are."

"Yep."

"I didn't know what to do, Shan."

"Yep."

"Al Warner's crazy."

"Yep."

At my house Dad's car was in the driveway.

"Okay then Shan, see you tomorrow?"

"Maybe," I said, already halfway up the drive.

I went straight up to my room and fell onto the bed, trembling, wishing I could erase the whole ugly scene from my mind. I hated Al Warner and all of them for what they'd done. I hated Rick for what he hadn't done. I hated Mandy for sucking up to Sue. But mostly I hated me because I wasn't brave. Not like Paul.

Now I could see how it would go; how I would be forced to be different. I couldn't be a normal person anymore, through no choice of my own. Maybe I wouldn't get beat up like Paul, but I had a feeling my responsibilities were different now. Were bigger. And harder.

It just proved again, sometimes you *do not have a choice*.

Chapter 32

A huge circle of green-gold light lit up the basin, at first appearing something like a flying saucer, so bright it made me squint. But as the light dimmed, it revealed three circles of people standing on prairie grass, one inside the next, all ages, sizes, races. They held hands, singing, some with strange voices. Spoken words in different languages floated through the air, but most often I heard someone somewhere saying, *It belongs to all of us.*

It belongs to all of us.
It belongs to all of us.
It belongs to all of us.

Then the light brightened again and dimmed, and

I realized it had a pulse. Even though the noises, voices, music were all over the place, there was an underlying throb to it, a soothing, mesmerizing, beautiful sound that matched the pulse of the green-gold glow.

But what's that? Smack in the middle of the circle, something in the shape of a large egg shone white and a hundred times brighter than anything else. No sooner did I see a set of arms moving out from the light, than a glittering flash caught my eye way over on the other side of the basin. It had fallen out of the sky, landed just outside the circle. I blinked. Blinked again. *What?*

Where it had touched the earth stood a young woman in a blue dress, who brushed herself off, wiped her eyes, then joined the outside circle. I tried to focus again on the glowing egg, but every few seconds came another flash, another arrival, two of these in wheelchairs. When a child appeared, he was pulled into the circle by an adult.

In the center ring, facing me, I could just make out a figure that moved toward the white light. Once more a set of arms rose out of the brilliance, and now I could see the shape of a head above those arms. Then everything was obliterated again by the brightness.

My eyes! Something strange was happening; they zoomed in and out, in and out, till I felt like barfing. I closed them, put my head down till it passed. *Dad! Dad! Where are you?*

When I looked up again I could see faces in the crowd, close up! I felt the ground. I hadn't moved, was still in the grass far away from the green-gold circles, yet I could scan their faces, could see that many looked like Ella, or had some other peculiar thing about them that told me they were "special." Only a very few looked "typical." Most of them seemed content, but some looked depressed or angry or sad. When their green-gold glowing pulsed to its brightest it was harder to make out what was what, but when it faded, and it seemed to be fading now for longer and longer stretches, I had more time to take in each face.

"Bonnie!" I gasped. There she was, large as life, sunglasses and all. She dropped them slightly, looked over them at the shining creature in the middle, whose outline now seemed quite human. Next to Bonnie I recognized the man from the mall, and a few feet from him was Bruce Kordinski, smiling and rocking in his wheelchair.

I looked back at the middleman just in time to see an older woman walk toward him, grinning from ear to ear. He embraced her, and then with super-strength, lifted her off her feet and said loudly, "Go out and balance the world." Then he tossed her, like a feather, high into the air, where she disappeared into a large cloud of shimmering colored speckles, just like I had seen in my little-kid dream. I began to see the pattern: as someone joined the outside circle, someone from the inside was tossed into the air. After a lot of people disappeared this way, it all felt very normal and somehow even beautiful, until I recognized the next person walking to the middle.

"*No-o-o-o-o-o!*" I screamed. "No, Ella-a-a-a! Come *ba-a-a-ck!*"

She'd brought me here. She had to get me home. By the time I'd leapt to my feet, she'd been tossed, and – *poof!* She was gone.

NO! No. No. No. No. NO-O-O-O-O-O! I'd had it. Had it! Had it!

I stomped down the embankment into the clearing, yelling my head off all the way.

"Ella-a-a-a-a-!!!"

I marched through them all, touched them. And still, no one noticed me!!!

I called Bonnie by name. I waved my arms in front of the man from the mall. I beeped the horn on Bruce's wheelchair. Still nothing. I was terrified to get any closer to the middleman, not knowing what he'd do to me. I spun around in circles till I thought I would faint. Just inside the inner circle I fell to my knees, shaking and crying. *Dad...Dad...come get me....Please....*

The middleman was gradually dimming, as though with each hug and toss, he was giving away a little piece of his light. "Go out and balance the world...Go out and balance the world...Go out and balance the world..."

I looked to the top of the basin where I'd come from, considered running back up to the forest. Behind the trees the sky was now a deep royal blue. The sun was on its way. There were no more flashes, no more arrivals; just one circle, not three. The middleman's radiance had died down so much I could now see he had his back to me and was actually quite short. And, of all things, was wearing shorts, a T-shirt, and a baseball cap.

Just then, behind me, a baby cried. I looked back in time to see someone throw it into the air. It flew gently toward the middle, and right over the man's head. My breath caught in my chest. It would surely crash to the ground. But the middleman's arms snapped into the air performing a perfect catch, like he had eyes in the back of his head.

He turned to me, his head down snuggling the child, the cap of his hat tipped across both of their faces. They glowed brightly together. "Go out and balance the world," he said softly into its ear. And just as he tossed it, I got a good look at the baby's sweet face, its reddish-brown hair.

"Gabriel!" I screamed, leaping up to grab him. I fell back to the ground in a heap. Millions of rainbow speckles snowed down around me. I sobbed uncontrollably into the grass.

"Shannon?"

Someone knew my name?

"Shannon?"

Slowly I lifted my head. Inches away, I saw his feet in a small pair of runners, then his shorts, covered by a familiar denim apron splotched with all colors of paint, and, finally, the face of the middleman revealed behind the last shimmers of radiance. I could barely speak.

"L-L-Lori?" I croaked.

"Hello Shannon," she said with the kind of smile you give someone you've been expecting. "Welcome to the circle."

Chapter 33

All along, after Gabe was born, different people had been coming by with hot meals for us, but one day a group from the church came with a carload of frozen casseroles to fill our big basement freezer. Thankfully, none of them said anything about God personally picking my parents. They just said they hoped we were doing well and that we were in their prayers. They seemed to think that would make a difference. I failed to see how prayers would ever make us happy again, but whatever.

We took some of these meals (thawed out, of course) to the hospital for Mom. She was glad to not have to eat the cafeteria food.

The day after Paul got beat up, as I watched her gobble down lasagne, I considered telling her and Dad about what had happened in the park. But I didn't. I was afraid they'd ban me from going there, and I was already banned from the mall. How would I ever see Rick? And anyway, I could tell by looking at them that they couldn't handle any more bad news.

After she ate, Dad stood on the other side of Mom's bed and he raised his eyebrows at her. Mom nodded and turned to me. Something was up. He cleared his throat. "Shannon, your mom and I have been thinking."

"Oh?" I could feel a lot of negativity in the air.

"As you know, we've been a little overwhelmed with life lately."

"Yeah?" I said.

"And you've been under some stress too, right?" He said this from behind Mom's back and then mouthed the name "Leo."

"I suppose," I replied, suspicious.

"So honey," Mom said, "Gabe and I are going to be here for a while yet, and, well…Denise Gormley has kindly…"

"I'M NOT GOING!" I yelled, jumping from my chair. "Dad, you already told her I wasn't going!"

"That was when we thought Gabe would be home. But he won't be. Not for a few weeks."

"Sweetheart," said Mom, "your dad and I need to be here with him all the time now. It's very tiring. Please understand."

They were just so totally thinking of themselves I could NOT believe it.

"But why a *church* camp," I blurted, "when I don't even believe in God?"

Admitting it was my last resort.

I expected a big stink, but it was like I'd said "Please pass the peas." They sat there in Mom's hospital room, like blobs, faces droopy and pale, the same way they'd been all week. Dad sighed deeply. "Shan, we've no energy to argue. On Sunday you go."

Chapter 34

Sleeping under the stars isn't exactly the best way to get a good night's sleep. The sun comes up way too early, and pretty soon it's pelting down on your sleeping bag so you're boiling to death, but your nose is practically freezing off your face. At five-thirty on Friday morning that's what I was feeling when I opened my eyes to a pink sky.

I rolled onto one side, pushed myself up on my elbow, and looked around. Only a few were stirring or talking quietly. Shelley was carrying logs to a fire pit. I gave a big stretch, arching back till I saw Sam's blonde hair sticking out of her sleeping bag and my heart stopped cold. My head was suddenly dizzy with images:

a forest, a pathway, glowing people, falling stars, Gabriel, Lori, and...*Ella!*

With a gasp I flipped over to find nothing but an open sleeping bag and her backpack.

"*Ellaaaa!*" I screamed. Girls jumped in their sleep and everyone yelled at me to shut up.

"Ella's gone!" I screamed again, and now everyone was sitting up. "Why won't you people listen to me?!?!"

"No she's not!" Tanya hollered from a patch of bushes just down the slope. "She's over here. She's just having a pee, for heaven's sake."

Everyone groaned. Hot as I was, I yanked my bag over my head to avoid the hateful glares. What was wrong with me?

But inside the darkness of my sleeping bag, everything came back, crystal clear. I fast-forwarded through it all, from the chase of Ella to the invisible wall, the great circle of people, those flying in, those thrown out, and finally, how Lori had hugged me and said, "I don't usually get to do this for people like you," and she lifted me high into the air and gave me a kiss and a gentle push, saying, "Go out and balance the world!"

I floated, weightless. Soon all I could see – eyes opened *or* closed – were the shimmering, comforting, colored speckles swirling around me. Then my nose was freezing and my body was boiling and I found myself on the top of Crocus Hill.

"Shannon, weck up!"

I peeked out and came nose-to-nose with Ella.

"Goo morning Sunsine," she grinned hugely. She patted my cheek with her so soft hand. I held it, squeezed it, made sure she was all in one piece.

"Ella," I whispered, "come closer."

When she did I asked, "Where'd you go last night?" She looked puzzled. "You know, when you went down the hill and followed that path. Remember?"

She went to stand up. I grabbed her arm, pulled her back. She looked confused.

"Last night, Ella, where'd you go?"

"Oooh," she said confidently, "I went to sleeeep." And then she laughed, pleased with herself for getting the answer right.

Chapter 35

The day before I was forced to leave for camp, Mom was let out of the hospital because her infection was better. She would still practically live there, but not in her own room, just a cot in a big room of cots near the Neonatal Unit. Gabe had stopped nursing again, so she was depressed.

At home Dad and I had let the gifts and cards pile up in the dining room, but I'd arranged them nicely on the table. Before she'd even looked at them, she told Dad and me to move them to the nursery and shut the door. Then she pumped some milk and took a long nap.

When she was up again, she said, "C'mon, missy, let's get you packed for camp."

"No. Not until I show you something."

I made her and Dad sit on the couch. I pulled out *Who's in Charge?* and turned to page 147 where Dianne Wimsworth clearly stated they were about to do the exact opposite of what she recommended in times of "family crises." I read this bit to their faces: "Family crises should be seen as opportunities to teach children about what they can expect in their own futures. They should learn how to cope with difficult events."

I tapped my finger on the page. "So you see, Mom and Dad, she did NOT say: 'Send your kid to camp.' I'm supposed to stay here and learn how to cope with difficult events."

"We're sorry, Shan," Dad said, an angry edge to his voice. "What's best for *us* is to have a couple of weeks on our own with Gabe. We need time to adjust to this new normal. The break would do you good. For all you know, it could turn out to be an amazing experience."

Right. Like that would ever happen.

I slammed Dianne Wimsworth shut and went upstairs to pack.

Chapter 36

Once the counselors said the sleeping outdoors part was over, I was first down the hill for breakfast. I kept my eyes peeled for Lori, but she didn't show. After we'd eaten, I asked Poobah where she was.

"She likes to sleep in," she replied. "Check her studio. She's always pleased to have a visitor."

I ran to the Gathering Hall and through to the back to knock on her door. Again. I tried the doorknob. Locked.

I spent the morning putting up a tepee with my cabin and two others. It was a rerun of First Nations

Day, but this time a grandmother elder and a couple of younger guys from a nearby reserve had come to take part. I was completely discombobulated and not of much help. All I could think about was my incredible dream. When the tepee was up we squeezed inside and the elder told us a story about a girl who'd had a vision, which the elder said is like having a bizarre dream! Even though the story-girl's was about animals and rocks and things, I was still freaked out about the coincidence.

Later, when we crossed the Bowl to go have lunch, I saw Lori just ahead, so I chased after her. "Lori! Hey Lori!" She turned to me and raised her eyebrows. "Yeth?"

For the first time I heard the slight lisp in her speech and I looked carefully at her mouth, how her tongue rested a tiny bit on her teeth. I saw her small nose and the very slight slant to her eyes. Maybe it was rude, but I reached out and she let me take her hands, and I turned them, palms up. There was the unbroken line. I looked her in the eye and said, "Go out and balance the world."

She looked *me* in the eye like I was a nutcase.

"You remember," I said, "last night, you welcomed me to the circle. It...it was some ritual thing. People came to you...people who were different...I mean, special...mentally...I mean, intellectually...they came to you and...you did something, like blessing them, or something that seemed wonderful...something that was good. You do remember, don't you?"

But she just turned away with a laugh, saying, "You're a very funny girl." And off she went.

So, now I was well and truly discombobulated. In the Mess Hall, when Brad scooted in right next to me on my bench, I didn't even notice until he grabbed the bannock off my plate and pretended to eat it. Unfortunately, this surprise made me scream in a juvenile way. Everyone around giggled, then someone pointed at the three gray hairs in his beard, they all began teasing him about it – also very juvenile. It was good that camp was about to end; their juvenility was rubbing off on me.

He dropped the bannock back on my plate and said quietly, "Meet me here at Free Time."

"Uh, okay. Why?"

"I've got something for you."

He left to get his lunch, and my heart thumped uncontrollably.

"Shannon's got a boyfriend, Shannon's got a boyfriend," chimed Patti. I rolled my eyes. The immaturity was unending.

Time passed like detention. He had something for me. A bracelet? A ring? I pictured him driving to Saskatoon to visit me, waiting for me to grow up just like that Elvis guy had to do with Priscilla on the Biography Channel.

And then finally, there I was, sitting across from him, with Mrs. Gormley spying on us from the kitchen across the way. Jeesh. I gave her the voo-doo evil eye and she pretended to be talking to the cooks.

"Sorry about the song thing," he began.

"Me too," I replied.

"I happen to agree with you. What you said about it."

Really? I thought.

"I think that song makes it all look too easy. It's completely misleading."

"Okay," I said, surprised, and therefore clueless about what to say next.

He rummaged in his backpack, then pushed a small photo album across the table. I flipped it open and found a card glued to the inside of the front cover. It read *Thank you Brad. We'll miss you!*

I flipped pages, photo by photo. Each was of a person who looked intellectually disabled. I stopped when I came to a man with a thick neck and slanted eyes that squinted with his smile.

"That's Jack," said Brad. "He has Downs."

"Yeah. I know."

"Yeah?"

"Yeah," I said.

I couldn't help compare his face to my brother's. It was as though Gabe had cousins everywhere.

Then, I got it.

"You know, don't you," I said. "You know about my brother."

"I do."

"Mandy? Did that Mandy tell you? She promised me…"

"No, no, not Mandy."

Mandy's mom was staring at us again. I shot her a shrivelling look, and her eyes dropped to the pot she was stirring.

"Mrs. Gormley, right?"

He nodded. "I knew you'd stayed the extra week thanks to her, so when you got so upset…well, I asked some questions."

I kept flipping through the album, not wanting him to see my face. Tears dropped on my lap. What if he thought I didn't want Gabe in my life? I kept my head down, my face burning with shame.

"Hey, hey," he whispered, "it's okay." He pulled some napkins out of the dispenser and handed them to me. I wiped my eyes. "Can I tell you something?"

I nodded.

"I used to work with these people in the photographs. We were at Newday Industries. I was there for three years. I loved it." He took the book back from me.

"This gal here, Becky, she has Downs, and you'd love her. She has such a great sense of humor; is surprisingly clever, actually. And this fellow, Robert, he took gold at the Special Olympics last year, in shot put, and he is truly an amazing athlete. Works out every day. Has Downs."

He pointed to a group picture, about twenty people with their arms around one another. "These are just a few of the folks I worked with. Many with Downs. I can honestly tell you that they – well, all the different people at Newday – are fantastic to be around. Like the rest of the world there are the odd exceptions – the disabled are allowed to be cranky too – but mostly you won't find a better group of buddies, or a place where you'll get very many more laughs a day."

I gave him a cold look. He flipped back to the picture of Jack.

"He's probably the guy I felt closest to," Brad went on, but now there was a crease between his eyebrows. "We just hit it off. I still drop in at his group home. He took pride in everything he did. The hardest worker you'll ever find. All the managers wanted him in their units – recycling, shrink-wrapping, envelope-stuffing.... Shannon, you aren't listening."

He sat back and sucked in his cheeks until his lips puckered. We stared each other down. Finally it came out of my mouth.

"I. Do. Not. Want. My brother. To be. An envelope-stuffer."

"Ah, I see." He drummed his fingers on the table. "Okay then. What's wrong with stuffing envelopes? People do it all over the world. It needs to be done."

"You know what I mean."

"No, actually, I don't."

"If Gabe ends up at Newday, then I'll be the one taking him there. If my parents die. When they die. And sometimes I'll have to be there, too, and hang around there, and be with those people...and I'm afraid..." My thought was interrupted by a big sob. I put my hand over my eyes, my head down.

"Let me tell you something," I heard him say. "When I first worked with *those people*, I wasn't paid. I was eighteen and in big trouble, and a judge had ordered me to do community service or go to jail." My face popped up in supreme amazement, which made him laugh. "Believe me, I didn't want to go to Newday. I'd wake up dreading it. Sometimes I thought jail would've been easier. I didn't know how to act with them. I'd always boasted that I was fearless, a tough guy, but there I was, scared to be with these gentle people. You could even say it disabled me. It took a while to stop seeing them through such fear-filled eyes."

I looked into those very same eyes and my armpits didn't itch. My heart didn't skip. He smiled and I became very calm. He had told me a big secret. Suddenly it felt safe and right to tell him a few of my own. I got up on my knees on the bench so I could lean over the table and speak quietly. Mrs. Gormley had left the kitchen, but who knew for how long. I began talking a mile a minute, pouring out the Six Bizarre Events, while he said things like, "Oh, yeah," and "Hmmm," and "R-r-right," and gradually got quieter and quieter till he didn't respond at all.

"And then last night," I blathered on, now in a whisper, no longer looking at Brad, not really aware of anything around me, "last night sleeping on Crocus Hill, when everyone had fallen asleep, Ella, that girl in my cabin with Down syndrome, she ran away, down the hill, and I was the only one who saw, so I followed her all night, over the prairie, into the forest, it was so frightening, until she led me to this great green-gold glowing circle of people, all disabled, you know, intellectually, even Bonnie was there, and the man from the mall, and his friends, and Paul's brother, and they all came into the circle on falling stars." I felt myself zoning out; swept up in my memories, now so vivid. "And then they all left the circle by being thrown into the air by…by…well… Lori…Lori the painter…who said to each person as she released them, 'Go out and balance the world!' Finally, it was my brother who landed in her arms, and I was terrified when she threw him up, up, till he disappeared into a million multi-colored, sparkling speckles, and then it was my turn. She threw me up and told me to balance the world, just like everyone else, and then I woke up sweating in my sleeping bag."

Silence.

In some distant place girls laughed. A screen door slammed. A spoon clanged against a pot. Someone cleared his throat. I blinked. Brad.

"Wow," he said, without moving so much as a hair. "Wow," he said again.

Wow? *Wow????* I felt barfy. What had I done?

I waited for him to say something more. And waited. And waited. He scratched his beard.

"Well," he cleared his throat again, "that was quite a dream."

"Wasn't a dream," I assured him. He nodded.

"C'mon Brad. Didn't you ever see those people at Newday do the glowing thing?"

"Can't say as I did." He cocked an eyebrow. "But that doesn't mean it didn't happen for you. In one way or another."

The dinner bell rang and he put the photos in his bag as I leapt to my feet.

"Brad…please don't tell anyone. About any of this. Please."

"I promise," he replied. "Go out and balance the world. I like that. An idea worth holding on to."

As we passed through the door going outside, I said, "There's something I wanna know. Why didn't anyone tell us that Lori has Downs?"

"What would be the point?"

"I don't know exactly," I replied, "it's just that maybe…"

"Listen, sometimes people want to know things just so they can show off what they know." He sounded annoyed. "But it doesn't mean anything. With Lori, what's important is she's an artist, a really fabulous painter, so most people don't notice her disability right away. If it was your brother, isn't that what you'd want for him?"

And I had to agree. It was.

✝✝✝

Lori the artist. The really fabulous painter. Here it was the last night of two weeks at camp, and I still hadn't seen her paintings!

Right after supper I took Ella by the hand and together we walked across the Bowl, through the empty Gathering Hall and knocked on the studio door. In a moment Lori opened it wearing a big grin, paintbrush in hand. Again I searched her face for some sign that she was the magical person I'd seen the night before. Nothing.

"Come in!" she exclaimed, smiling hugely as usual.

The room was large with windows down one side, so there was lots of light. Art supplies were everywhere. Ella immediately began touching things.

"No, no!" said Lori, wagging her finger.

Leaning against the walls were large canvases, mostly paintings of huge, bright flowers, and some abstracts too. The colors were gorgeous.

"You're a fantastic artist," I told her, and she beamed.

"Beee-ooo-tifo," added Ella.

At the far end of the room, next to a table of paint tubes and brushes, there was an easel holding up another large canvas.

"Is this what you're working on now?"

"Yeth," she replied.

I walked around to the other side of the easel to check it out.

I just about keeled over.

Some would think it was just "abstract" art, but not me. Lori had painted a large, glowing, green circle. All around it gold streaks shot into the circle from a dark blue background. In the center a single, bright white star radiated, and around it, she had just begun to painstakingly paint masses of tiny dots. Speckles. In every color imaginable.

"This is my dream," I said under my breath. "This is my dream," I said to Lori. "You *were* there."

Lori looked at Ella and shrugged her shoulders.

Ella stared at the painting, ran her fingers over the speckles and said, "It belongs to aw of us."

"What?" I said. "What did you say?"

"It belongs to aw of us."

"What does, Ella?"

She tilted her head, looked at me quizzically, like I should know the answer. With her finger she drew a circle in the air and said, "Why, da world, of course."

I looked into her lovely, almond-eyed face and everything became absolutely crystal clear.

"Of course, Ella," I said. "Of course."

†††

Later that night, after campfire, I told Brad all about the painting and with big eyes, he agreed to go with me to Lori's studio to see it. But when we got there she was gone, and so was all her stuff.

"It was here. Really. I swear. "

"I believe you, Shan," he replied, which was a relief. "You saw what you saw. Come here. Sit down."

He gestured to a couple of stray chairs, and we sat in the near dark of the empty hall.

"I've been thinking a lot about your brother," he said. "A child like him can make you see people, I mean typical people, in a different light. Gabe has the power to bring out the best in everyone around him."

"I beg to differ," I said. I told him about Paul Kordinski being beaten up; what they said about his disabled brother. How even Mandy Gormley, who was in love with church camp and was all Christian and stuff, had stuck up for Sue instead of Paul. "So you see," I told him, "it's not all rosy like you're saying. Sometimes kids like Gabe actually bring out the worst in people."

Brad crossed his arms, leaned back and looked at the

227

ceiling. While he was thinking it over I told him, "When we get home from Camp Outlook, I've decided I won't be friends with Mandy anymore."

"Well, you could do that," he said, "but then she'll never know Gabe. Maybe if she'd known someone like him she would've seen Sue's behavior differently. And she would've stuck up for Paul, just like you did."

I stared at my feet, unable to meet his eyes. Moments passed.

"Ah, I see," he said. "Well, I suppose you were in a dangerous situation, really." He stood up. "Guess we'd better go. It'll soon be lights-out."

We strolled out the door and stood on the steps in the cool night air. I was looking for something to say, a way to explain why I couldn't have done anything to help Paul. Why I couldn't stop Al Warner.

"Have a good life," Brad said with a smile, and patted me on the back.

"You too," I said. He bounded down the steps, carrying his guitar. Then he stopped and turned around. "Look Shannon, I know you didn't get the baby you wanted, and I understand why everything's broken with you and God." He looked away briefly, like he didn't know if he should go on. But then he did. "I just think it's interesting that for me, it's the Newday people who *connected* me to God; they showed me everything I had waiting inside me to give to others. Without Newday, I'm not sure I'd ever have found my true calling."

"But that's you," I replied.

"Yes, I suppose so. But you, you've had something special. For me it's just been an everyday experience that woke me up. For you it's been something mystical. Lucky you."

With that, he swung his guitar case across his back and disappeared into the night.

Chapter 37

When I hold Gabriel and look into his face for long stretches of time, I wonder if I'm right or wrong about God. I can't make up my mind. What I do know for absolute sure is something important happened at Camp Outlook. Something huge and totally mysterious and completely beautiful. Maybe even something mystical, but I don't know if it had anything to do with God. I do know it had everything to do with Ella. And Gabriel. And I know it changed me forever.

I used to think he was the only needy one; that he would always need my mom and dad and me to survive. But now I know it's actually the three of us who need

Gabe. We need him every single day. He is the perfect baby for us and we would be totally and completely lost without him.

He's three months old now and smiles like he swallowed the sun. And he's *a big* eater, so mom nurses him a zillion times a day. Therefore he poops often, which is when I sometimes help to change his cute, stinky little bum.

The good news is he'll get his heart surgery before Christmas because he's healthy now. We aren't as worried about it because we joined a support group where all the families have a child with Downs. Some of those kids had the same operation and all of them turned out one hundred percent okay.

Because of the group, I have a new friend. Her name is Cynthia and she has a new brother with Downs too, as well as five other sisters, if you can believe it. (Dad says they're good Catholics.) She lives only two blocks away, so it's perfect.

Mandy and I are still friends, just not best friends, for now. After camp was finished I invited her to come over and play with Gabe, and I could tell she loved him. I asked her if she'd managed to get through the whole two weeks without blabbing about our abnormal family to anyone.

"I kept it to myself," she replied.

"Really?" She looked hurt by my disbelief. "I'm sorry, but really??"

"I thought about it a lot, why you wouldn't trust me, and remembered what happened with Al Warner, how I got you in trouble with him. You were right. Sometimes I say too much."

"Well, I should never have made you promise to keep Gabe a secret in the first place. There's nothing wrong with being abnormal."

And I meant it. I'm with Gabe a lot, and every day I notice something new and amazing. Yes, some things are like having a typical baby, but there are major differences, too. Dressing him is like putting clothes on a wet noodle because he has less muscle than regular babies. It's a lot of work for him to lift his arms or legs. As Dad says, gravity is not his friend. Because he works harder to do some things, he's more tired. The physiotherapist showed us how to do certain things when we play with him to build up his muscles. And the speech therapist showed us how to massage his face in certain particular ways to strengthen his face muscles.

Gabe has a lot of appointments. Sometimes Mom and Dad complain about being constantly on the run, but this is very minor and we all know it. Our home has

become a happier and happier place, even though sometimes I still look at my brother with fear-filled eyes. This
happens if I think about when my parents die, or even
when I die. I don't want Gabe ever to be alone.

Walking to school one day at the beginning of grade
eight, I was thinking these kinds of sad thoughts about
my parents dying when Paul Kordinski came to mind.
I wondered if he worried about the same things; if he
worried about who'd care for his brother. At recess I went
looking for him. He was in the Science Club greenhouse,
dropping seeds into paper cups.

"Hi Paul." He lifted his eyes, and I could see he was
bewildered. We'd never talked before.

"Hi," he said.

"I'm Shannon James."

"I know who you are." He turned his back on me
and reached for some more cups. I could feel my face
going red.

"I just wanted to say that was terrible, what happened in the park during the summer. I'm really, really
sorry."

He shuffled the cups on the table, refusing to turn
around.

"I should've done something more to help you that
day."

"No worries," he said curtly.

"You were so brave, Paul." He didn't respond. "Also, I wanted to tell you that in July my parents had a baby, and…well…I became the sister of someone who has Down syndrome."

He swung around and his eyes locked on mine. "Why are you telling me this?"

"Isn't it obvious?" I replied.

"Listen, if you think you understand me, or my life, or my brother's, just because you've been around a Downs baby for a few weeks, you'd be wrong."

And with that he pushed past me and headed out the door.

Chapter 38

On the last morning of Camp Outlook I woke before everyone else and rolled around uncomfortably in my sleeping bag, feeling incredibly sad. I thought about Lori and her green-glow painting, and then about Brad. I would miss him for a while. I thought about him almost going to jail; how he might have turned out totally different if he'd been made to go there instead of to Newday. I imagined telling Mandy his incredible story; the amazement on her face. But when he'd mentioned the judge and jail, he'd trusted me. He thought I was one of those people who wouldn't blab "just to show off what they know."

There was no good reason to tell anybody what I knew.

He'd also had courage to tell me that. He couldn't predict what I'd think of him. But sometimes there were things that needed to be told; things that took courage to tell.

The rest of the girls began to stir and soon the cabin was filled with the excitement of packing up to go home.

Breakfast was extremely noisy with so many people running around, saying good-bye, getting cell phones back from Poobah, getting text addresses from everyone, and, of course, getting autographs. I'd left my autograph book in the cabin because I didn't want anyone to flip to the back and read my Bizarre Events pages. Patti and Regan handed me theirs, so I signed them, in between bites of scrambled eggs. In one I wrote *As long as grapes grow on a vine, you'll always be a friend of mine,* in the other, *Yours till Niagara Falls! Ha ha.*

Tanya had Ella by the hand and was over talking to Mrs. Gormley, who then went into the kitchen office and came back with a small stack of notepaper and a stapler. They stapled the paper together and Ella happily presented us with her new autograph book. "Sign peas. Sign peas." And we all did. When she got to me I wrote:

If I were a head of cabbage I'd cut myself in two.
To all my friends I'd give a leaf, but I'd save my heart for you

I read it aloud to her, but she was completely confused.

"It means I like you, Ella. It means we're friends."

"Fends. We are fends."

She and I walked back to the cabin together, arm in arm, then finished up our packing along with everyone else. I listened closely to the conversation and looked for my opportunity. Finally Sophia said, "When I get home there's going to be a million e-mails and texts waiting."

Then Patti said, "Me, too. And I've *soooo* got to get new clothes for school."

"When I get home there's going to be a new baby in the house."

The cabin went quiet. I'd said it a lot louder than I'd meant to, so everybody was gawking at me. After a moment Regan said, "Really? That's so great."

"You never mentioned it before," went Patti. "Whose baby is it?"

"My mom's, of course…and Dad's, too."

Everyone stopped what they were doing.

"Well, was he just born or what?" asked Sophia.

"Not exactly. He's almost a month old. His name's Gabriel and he's actually still in the hospital, but he'll be out soon."

"Baby," said Ella as she sat down on her bunk. "Beautifo baby."

"Yes. He's beautiful, Ella. And he has Down syndrome."

"Like me," she said, matter-of-factly.

"Just like you." I hesitated to look up. When I did I could see that none of the girls knew quite what to say. But Patti broke the ice. "If Gabriel is as nice as Ella, you're really lucky."

Ella's face lit up like she'd won a medal, and we all broke up.

Then Tanya said, "And Gabriel's lucky to have you for a sister."

"Thank you," I replied, and stuffed my autograph book into my bag. Someone knocked on the door and opened it. Ella's mom. Here a half hour early. Ella ran to her, threw her arms around her, and her mom buried her face in Ella's neck. When she looked up she had tears in her eyes.

"Have you had a good time?" she asked her daughter.

"Oh, yes, Mom. Oh, yes," she said, then went around introducing her mom to each of us.

We followed them out into the Bowl to say our good-byes. Ella's mom cried as each girl gave Ella a big hug, then hurried back to the cabin to finish packing. I was last, and we shared a long squeeze that meant I couldn't swallow because I had such a gigantic rock-hard lump in my throat. Finally I croaked something to her mom.

"My brother has Downs," I said.

"Oh," she replied, "how old is he?"

"He was just born a month ago."

"Were your parents expecting it?"

"No."

"Ah, I've been where you are. It's hard right now, isn't it."

I nodded. She bent down and gave me a hug. She looked directly in my eyes, and I noticed how wrinkled they were, especially when she smiled. "There are always going to be days that are hard, even harder than now, but I can promise you there will be many, many more that will take your breath away." She squeezed my shoulders, stood up and took Ella's hand. They walked away, swinging their arms between them. My heart felt huge and sore, wondering how the rest of their lives would go.

I watched them until the last possible moment and caught myself whispering to Ella's back, "Go out and balance the world," believing she'd somehow hear me. My words seemed to echo in the Bowl and soon, instead of my voice, it was Lori's I heard. *Go out and balance the world. Go out and balance the world. Go out and balance the world.* Then I realized something: Lori had given me the exact same blessing as Gabe and Ella and everyone else.

Standing in the middle of Camp Outlook, in the center of the circle of trees glowing green in the morning sun, and not caring who thought I was crazy, I shouted it straight up into the sky, "Go out and balance the world!"

This time the words were meant for me.

Just for my own self.

Chapter 39

Every time I thought about Sue Morrison and what she'd said to Paul about his brother, I got a sharp pain my gut. She was so totally clueless about what it feels like deep inside when someone you love is disabled. I got myself so worked up again I just wanted to punch her lights out. In the end I didn't punch her lights out. I did something much better.

I hadn't told my parents about Paul getting beaten up, but when he had talked to me as though having a brother with Downs was nothing to complain about, and that I'd never understand his situation, I didn't know what to think. So in October, I told my parents everything, including the terrible things Sue had said to Paul, and also how she'd made fun of the man with Downs at the Food Court.

"Sounds like Paul has really been hurt," said Dad. "It might be a while before he'll let you be his friend. As for Sue, well, sometimes parents don't talk to their kids about people with intellectual disabilities, because it makes them uncomfortable. They don't know much about it."

"But I've met Sue's mother a few times," Mom said, "and she seems like a kind person. I can't see Sue being so different."

I rolled my eyes. Sometimes adults just didn't get how kids think.

"Mom, she was mean to Paul so she'd be noticed by certain particular people."

"If that's the case, then maybe she doesn't really believe what she's saying."

The next day, after school, I was doing homework and Mom was nursing Gabe when she said, "Your dad and I have come up with a plan."

When she first explained it I thought it was a horrible idea, but eventually I agreed it was worth a try.

So that's how Sue and her mom ended up on our doorstep the following weekend. Sue seemed nervous, like she really didn't want to be there. She looked lost without her cigarette and her gang of cool friends. As Mrs. Morrison came in she said, "What a pleasant surprise, Nora. We'd heard about your baby, but didn't expect to be on your list of visitors."

"Well, we just love showing off our handsome son," said Mom.

Mrs. Morrison passed a gift bag to my dad and said, "Congratulations."

"You shouldn't have," said Dad, "but thank you."

"Look at him," she cooed. "May I?"

"Of course," Mom said, and passed Gabe to her.

We sat in the living room, and Mom poured juice as Dad passed a plate of cookies. Mom told her C-section story for the billionth time, including every gory detail of the belly stapling. This time, I'm sure it was just to see Sue wince, which she did, but she also looked genuinely amazed to hear what Mom had gone through.

In a little while, it was time for my part in my parents' grand plan. I went over and took Gabe from Sue's mom. I gave him a cuddle and a kiss and then, without even asking her if she wanted him, I put him right into Sue's arms. I sat up close to them and stroked my brother's hand. There was a lot I wanted to say to Sue, but I had to trust that Gabe knew what to do.

He stared intensely into her face and then gave her one of his killer smiles. She couldn't help but smile back and say, "He is *soooo* cute." He grabbed at her nose and looked at her again, oh so sweetly. Then Sue reached for his hand and tried to get him to hold her finger. Even though his soft muscles made it hard for him to make a fist, Gabriel wrapped his fingers around hers and squeezed till she let out a laugh.

That's when I believed it, with all my heart and soul: My incredible brother was balancing the world.

Acknowledgments

Camp Outlook was inspired by Tori, my late daughter, and the fascinating disability community of which we became members. It was also inspired by my fond memories of the real Camp Outlook, where I met a "Bonnie" and a "Jesus-Brad."

I will be forever indebted to Scott Treimel for his belief in this book, and his immensely helpful review of several drafts of the manuscript. John Cusick also provided critical feedback on a near-final version. Beverly Brenna, Leona Theis and Arthur Slade helped push it along in its early stages. Thanks to these folks, when publisher Margie Wolfe called to request *Camp Outlook*, she said it was ready to go and would be in bookstores within a few months! I want to thank Margie for loving *Camp Outlook* and for not making me rewrite it *again!*

That said, I was so pleased to have the astute eye of one of the most respected editors in the business, Kathryn Cole, to do some tweaking and polishing. *Camp Outlook* was a tricky story to tell. Kathryn's faith in the premise was encouraging.

I appreciate the financial support of the Saskatchewan Arts Board and the Canada Council for the Arts. Many programs of the Saskatchewan Writers Guild have been of help over the years, in particular the Writers' Retreats and the John V. Hicks Manuscript Award, both of which energized my writing.

Camp Outlook is my dad's kind of book and I wish I'd thought to give him the manuscript before his passing. He would have seen his guidance in it. My mom and my in-laws continue to be the best parents an artist could ask for.

Finally, I'm blessed to live with two creative souls, Art and Tanaya, who make my own creative life possible. They both deserve more attention from me than they sometimes receive, but understand that "Mommy has to work to make the money that buys the candy."

About the Author

Brenda Baker is an award-winning writer, performer and recording artist from Saskatoon. Her unique creative life includes attaining a BFA in visual art; coast-to-coast appearances and two CD releases as a songwriter for adults; a TV series, three CD releases and regular concerts as a children's entertainer; and a Saskatchewan Book Award for Fiction for her collection of short stories, *The Maleness of God*. Brenda began her journey as a mother in 2003, but continued to pursue her artistic interests whenever possible. She launched Nexstage Live Music Performance Coaching to help emerging artists develop their live shows. For nine years Brenda has been the Founding Director of

Kids of Note, the hit performing group for children, with and without disabilities, who love to sing. *Camp Outlook* is her first novel. Before publication it was given a John V. Hicks Manuscript Award. Brenda's children's story, *Tiny Teresa Twiddle*, won a Saskatchewan Literary Award.

Brenda lives in Saskatoon with writer Arthur Slade and their daughter Tanaya.

Visit Brenda online at BrendaBaker.com.